"STEPHIE YATES, PRIVATE EYE."
JORDAN SMILED.

For once Stephie didn't rise to the bait. Let Jordan tease her. She didn't care. If she found out who had killed Matt and made sure his killer got charged with vehicular homicide that was all she wanted. Maybe she had been right when she said there was a ghost among them. Maybe Matt's ghost was refusing to let her rest until she brought that drunk driver to justice.

Some people can't take a hint, thought the murderer, regarding Stephie through dangerously narrowed eyes. The problem was she didn't know enough to back off. She needed a lesson. It would be awfully convenient if she would disappear, like through a trapdoor. Too bad it didn't work that way. If Stephie was going to disappear, somebody was going to have to help her along. But that shouldn't be hard at all. There was bound to be some way or other to get at her without anybody knowing . . .

FLASHPOINT

JANICE HARRELL

AN ARCHWAY PAPERBACK
Published by POCKET BOOKS

New York   London   Toronto   Sydney   Tokyo   Singapore

AN ARCHWAY PAPERBACK *Original*

An Archway Paperback published by
POCKET BOOKS, a division of Simon & Schuster Inc.
1230 Avenue of the Americas, New York, NY 10020

ISBN: 0-671-75417-3

First Archway Paperback printing May 1992

10 9 8 7 6 5 4 3 2 1

AN ARCHWAY PAPERBACK and colophon are registered trademarks of Simon & Schuster Inc.

Cover art by Broeck Steadman

Printed in the U.S.A.

IL 6+

1

The house hummed with energy and noise—the chatter of shifting groups, the clink of glasses, and over it all the thump and whine of loud music. That was probably why, when the police asked about him later, so many kids couldn't remember when they had last seen Matt.

Suddenly a loud screech blared from the speakers and the music stopped.

"You sat on the turntable, Dennis," cried Melissa Lamm. "It's broken."

"I did?" A goofy-looking boy with frizzy hair jumped up suddenly.

"Hey, and you're only drinking apple juice." The girl in black was amused. "You don't have any excuse. Oh, well, not to worry. I've got a boom box in the car."

The broken turntable didn't seem to make much difference in the noise level.

"I think this is the best party you've ever had," someone yelled in the host's ear.

"Whah?" J. J. Cochran yelled back as a flashbulb went off in his face. "Will you cut that out, Melissa?" he yelped. "I'm seeing blue dots all over the place."

"This new camera is, like, incredible," said Melissa, still peering through the viewfinder. "It's completely automatic. Absolutely impossible to mess up."

"It's perfect for you, then," said Jordan McGuire. When she looked at him in surprise, he backed off. "Just kidding." He smiled.

"It's even got its own clock," Melissa went on happily. "It stamps the time on every picture I take."

J.J.'s parents were out of town for the weekend. They had told him it would be okay to have a party as long as he made sure nobody threw up on their new sofa. To his horror, J.J. saw Matt Howell—by anyone's standards the drunkest guy at the party—heading toward the white sofa. "Get away from that sofa, Matt!" J.J. yelled. "Don't sit there! Don't even think of it!"

"Who's gonna stop me?" muttered Matt.

Stephie Yates stepped in and took charge. "Come on, Matt," she said. "Let's get you something to eat."

Matt let Stephie lead him into the kitchen. It was quieter there and she hoped he would get into less trouble. She set about making him a sandwich with the vague hope that it would soak up some of the liquor in his stomach. The light directly overhead shone down on the loose curls of his dark hair, casting his eyes into shadow and calling attention to his high, broad cheekbones as he glowered at her. His shirt was open at the neck and the one-of-a-kind Navaho bead necklace Jordan had brought him from an Arizona vacation made a slash of color across his white throat, the tiny, close-packed beads winking under the kitchen light, azure, yellow, and red in narrow bands. The wild and alien bit of jewelry seemed to fit him in a careless, pagan sort of way. Then she remembered what her grandmother used to say—pretty is as pretty does.

"Eat," said Stephie, abruptly pushing the sandwich toward him.

"Not hungry," he mumbled. "Need another beer." He bent to get a can from the open cooler on the floor. His pale, almost white, jeans were slashed across one thigh and decorated with elaborate figures in black and red marker. Stephie herself had added a red heart to the design. Above it Matt had printed in block letters—Save Me from Myself. The motto suddenly seemed wildly appropriate as she watched him tear the flip top off the beer can.

"Put that down. You don't need another beer."

"Everybody thinks they can tell me what to do. You all want to control me. Everybody around here's on some power trip—you, Jordan, my mom. Everybody. Well, let me tell you, nobody bosses this guy. Matt Howell flies alone. Like the eagle, man." His upper lip lifted in a smile that was like a sneer. He poured an amber stream of beer into his open mouth and let it slide down his neck.

"That's disgusting," said Stephie. "Matt, put that can down."

"You think I'm going to let a girl tell me what to do?" He steadied himself against the kitchen table.

"Put it down this minute," she yelled, "or we're through."

"Oh, come on, Stephie. Don't be that way." The

corners of his mouth turned down as if he were a hurt child. "Lay off. I'm just trying to have a good time."

Stephie felt her heart twist inside her. Why did he have to do this to her? Lately, it was as if Matt were purposely trying to blot out the nice guy he used to be. He had started reading comic books about weird, sinister superheroes and had plastered his room with quotes like "Man is a rope stretched between the animal and the Superman—a rope over an abyss." What did that mean, for heaven's sake?

She met his glassy eyes and took a deep breath. He stank of beer. "You're drunk."

"Nah!" He wiped his mouth clumsily.

"You're so drunk you don't even know it," she cried. "You think I like it that everybody feels sorry for me? You think it's fun watching you make an idiot of yourself? I've had enough. Go ahead—drink yourself to death if you want. We're finished."

"Hey!"

"I'm not kidding, Matt. I've had it. This is it. The end." She swallowed. "I can't take it anymore. I swear, I don't care if I ever see you again."

He clutched at her shoulder and spun her around. "Don't be mad, Stephie." His voice was low. "You know I love you."

"Excuse me. This is not my idea of love," she said coldly and pulled away from him.

As she stumbled to the powder room and splashed water on her face a kaleidoscope of crazy memories wheeled through her mind almost making her dizzy. She remembered Matt's eyes, intent on the sky, the day he taught her to fly a kite, the roughness of his fingers on her cheek, the sweetness of his smile. But he'd changed. He acted as if he didn't like himself

4

anymore. Maybe that was why he had gotten so disgustingly drunk. She didn't care anymore now. She was fed up with making excuses for him and tired of trying to understand what was going on with him.

Stephie wasn't sure how long she stood there. A damp strand of dark hair clung to her neck as she patted her face dry with a tiny embroidered guest towel, but she scarcely noticed. She was wondering how she'd get home. She could call her mother, but the problem was her mother was going to be upset when she realized how wild the party had been. Maybe it would be better to ask someone else. She took a few ragged breaths as she watched in the mirror the tanned oval of her face blur with tears. She didn't care how mad her mother was, she decided. She wanted to go home—now.

Stephie called home from the study, but there was no answer. She glanced in the open door of the kitchen and saw that Matt had gone. Sniffling, she went into the kitchen and sat down at the table. She didn't want anyone to see her crying. She shook open the evening newspaper that was lying there and pretended to read it, trembling with emotion still. Matt claimed to be so independent! She wished he could see himself. He hooked his thumbs in the belt loops of his jeans, just the way Jordan did, and for weeks during the summer he had gone around saying, "No problem" just because Jordan did. Of course, if she had pointed this out, he would have denied it. Jordan could have made him put down that beer if he wanted. If Jordan said "jump" all Matt ever wanted to know was "how high?" They were like two sides of the same penny, inseparable.

Matt was still showing off, she thought bitterly. It

was as if he were ten instead of sixteen. He wanted to look tough and dangerous like some doomed rock star, but it was all phony and stupid. She folded up the newspaper and stared at it without seeing it. She was glad to be rid of him, she told herself. She really was.

Brad Elkins stumbled into the kitchen just then, followed by J.J. and Dennis Bradley. "Call nine one one," Brad ordered, "it's Matt!"

"Matt?" Stephie repeated.

Brad vomited into the kitchen sink.

"What's happened?" she cried. "Is he hurt? Has he passed out?"

Brad turned on the water, wiped his hand clumsily over his mouth, and stared wide-eyed at her. "He's dead. Somebody ran over him."

J.J. grabbed the phone off the wall. "Are you sure, man?" he yelled.

"Where is he?" cried Stephie.

"Don't let her go outside!" warned Brad.

Stephie was conscious of a faint roaring in her ears. Dennis held her back and kept her in the kitchen. She could hear J.J. giving the nine one one operator the address. "Hang on, Stephie," Dennis said. "The ambulance'll be here in a minute."

She sagged in his arms. "They'll fix him up, won't they?"

Dennis met Brad's eyes and shook his head. "No," he said quietly. "He's gone."

Her stomach contracted in sudden pain. Matt was dead, and nobody would let her see him. What was it Brad had said? Run over? She felt sick and lowered herself into a chair. Her gaze fell on the sandwich she had made for Matt—the top slice of bread was already curling at the edges as it dried. She put her face in her hands and began to cry.

It turned out later that Stephie was the only person who was able to say definitely when she had last seen Matt. She could hardly have forgotten it, she thought miserably. After all, she had told him that she never wanted to see him again.

The day of Matt's funeral the grass was parched from a long drought and the flowers that blanketed the coffin lost their color in the glare.

The murderer took in the crowd that had gathered around the green canopy and was pleased that almost everyone was wearing sunglasses. A good thing since that made it impossible to tell who was crying and who wasn't. No one suspected, not even the police, that Matt's death hadn't been an accident.

Pulse steady. Palms cool. I'm CIA material, thought the murderer. And a genius at improvisation, face it. Because, in a sense, Matt's death had been an accident. It certainly hadn't been planned. Things had gotten a little out of hand, that was all. It had been Matt's fault—he was the one who was to blame.

A glance at the flower-draped coffin gave the murderer a cold feeling in the pit of the stomach. This could mean jail for a long, long time if the truth came out. There was no reason it should come out, though. No one could possibly know that someone had left the party for a few important minutes—just long enough to drag Matt into the center of the driveway and run the truck over him. There were no fingerprints. No telltale clues. No one was even looking for clues. That's why it was the perfect crime. Well, not a crime actually because it was just such a spur-of-the-moment thing. Pulse steady, palms cool. Right.

Stephie was vaguely aware that a large crowd was gathered around the green canopy where she sat in a folding metal chair beside Matt's family. J.J. and Jordan were standing just behind her, scarcely recognizable in their sunglasses. J.J.'s build was odd in a suit. His overdeveloped shoulders strained against the fabric of his gray flannel jacket. Jordan, tall and slender in a navy blazer, looked as if he had stopped by the funeral on his way to a sailing regatta. The sun winked off his blazer buttons and reflected blankly on his rimless sunglasses.

Matt's mother was crying in gulping, ugly sobs. If only Mrs. Howell hadn't asked her to sit with the family, thought Stephie unhappily. She glanced down at the white band of flesh around her finger where her class ring had been. Mrs. Howell had asked Stephie to put her class ring in the coffin with Matt. The whole idea had struck Stephie as sick, but she couldn't figure out a way to refuse. She was still angry at Matt, she realized. It was unfair of him to die before they had a chance to make up.

The priest's voice recalled her to the present with a start. "We commend to Almighty God our brother Matthew, and we commit his body to the ground; earth to earth, ashes to ashes, dust to dust. The Lord bless him and keep him."

Half the town had turned out for the funeral out of sympathy for the family. A good smattering of Matt's teachers were there and all of his friends. J.J. fished for a handkerchief in his coat pocket. "Jeez, this is grim. I don't know how much more I can take."

"Pull yourself together, man," whispered Jordan.

"Matt wouldn't want us to be down. You know that. Remember how he said he wanted everybody to have a big dance and barbecue at his funeral?"

J.J. wiped his eyes. "Yeah, but jeez," he whispered, "he wasn't serious. He never figured—I just can't believe it. It's like something you read about in the paper, not something that really happens to you. People aren't supposed to die before they get out of high school."

"May his soul and the souls of all the departed, through the mercy of God, rest in peace. Amen," intoned the priest.

After the graveside service was over, Matt's dad and his uncle supported Mrs. Howell back to the long black limousine.

Melissa ran up to J.J. and Jordan, her frothy blond hair and red-framed sunglasses oddly out of place with her somber gray flannel dress. "It's awful," she choked. "I can't believe that he's really gone. Like, it just doesn't seem real, you know? It's more like I'm watching it on a video or something and tomorrow I'll wake up and he'll be here."

"I know." Jordan squeezed her. "But at least we've got each other."

"You're right." She cast a glance over her shoulder. "Poor Stephie. It's awful for her. Rachel, too. She took off just now without a word."

When Stephie heard her name she raised her head instinctively and saw her friends standing in a cluster nearby. Suddenly she couldn't wait to get away from the green canopy with the flower-draped casket beneath it. Tears were streaming down her cheeks as she struggled awkwardly past Matt's relatives. Finally she reached her friends. "They put my ring in his coffin," she whispered.

Melissa gripped her hand. "Oh, Stephie."

"I keep thinking if I hadn't had that stupid party, he'd still be alive," said J.J.

"We can't blame ourselves," said Jordan. "It was awful but it wasn't anybody's fault."

"You're right," said J.J. "We've got to quit being morbid." He blew his nose loudly.

"I have to get on home," said Jordan. "My mom wants me to take a ham over to Matt's house."

"Sure." Stephie hesitated a moment. Suddenly all her friends were strangers to her—those blank faces, gray clothes, and sunglasses. Shivering, she stumbled blindly to her car.

2

A couple of weeks after Matt's funeral the long summer drought, which had lasted well into fall, turned to mist and rain. When Stephie got to school early for Quiz Bowl practice one morning, a constant drizzle veiled the low lights at the school's front entrance. To her surprise Dennis was already in the library when she walked in. Beads of moisture from the damp were still glistening on his frizzy hair. "Hi!" he said. He reddened when she smiled at him.

Stephie perched on a table and took a look around her. The bright lights of the library shone on stacks of books and filmstrips, and on the colorful wall posters and bulletin boards with their notices about opportunities for seniors. She felt impatient with the hokey cheerfulness of the room. She had come in to practice early that morning only because she was having trouble sleeping. Matt's death filled her mind until she thought her head might burst.

11

"Whatever happened with the police investigation, Dennis?" she asked abruptly.

"Run that by me again," he said.

No one could have been more different from Matt, she decided. Dennis's neck was too long, his ears stuck out slightly, and he smiled too much to be cool.

"The police investigation," she repeated. "Nobody ever told me what happened. My mother hid the newspapers from me. Now that I'm trying to find out exactly what happened I can't get anyone to talk about it. Nobody will tell me anything."

"The police said it was an accident. Do you really need to know more than that? It'll just get you upset."

"I'm not going to faint or anything. Don't worry."

He closed his history book. "A pickup truck ran over him. The light isn't great out at J.J.'s, as you know. There's no street lamp, just the light over the front door of the house. I guess the driver of the pickup didn't see Matt. Then, I guess, when he realized what had happened he panicked. The cops found the truck just a little way past J.J.'s house. It had been run off the road and into a ditch."

"You're trying to tell me it was a hit-and-run accident?"

"I guess." Dennis shrugged. "Maybe he was so drunk he didn't even know he hit anybody."

Stephie could almost see the truck rolling over Matt's body and nausea rose in her throat. Perhaps she shouldn't have asked Dennis to tell her what happened after all. She had thought she was ready to talk about it, but maybe not.

"Turns out the truck belonged to a senior named Tony Dickson," Dennis went on, "but he wasn't driving it. He was upstairs at J.J.'s with his girlfriend at the time. His girlfriend backs him up, and Sumir

Kumar was sitting on the stairs writing a computer program. He swears Tony never passed him. Tony was just stupid enough to leave the key in the truck. Some drunk must have seen the key and decided to take it for a spin."

"I can't believe they couldn't find out who it was."

Dennis shrugged. "I know. They went over the whole truck for fingerprints, but the only ones they came up with were Tony's. He had the steering wheel wrapped in tape so they couldn't get anything there."

Stephie shook her head as if that could clear away the bloody images in her mind. "It *had* to be someone at the party. J.J. lives way out of town. It's not like somebody could have just happened to pass by and decided to borrow the truck. Nobody passes by that house. It's out in the middle of nowhere."

"Yeah, but I don't think we're ever going to find out who. Didn't the police ask you a bunch of questions?"

"I guess. Yeah, sure they did. But those first couple of days after it happened are pretty much a blur, to tell you the truth."

"Well, they grilled everybody. I don't know what it was like when they talked to you, but with me it was like the closest thing I ever hope to get to a third degree. Scared my parents to death. They wanted to get me a lawyer. But, hey, I didn't know anything. Nobody knew anything. I heard they came up with zip."

Dennis stopped talking when he noticed J.J. blocking the doorway to the library. He was relieved and obviously hoped J.J. would change the subject. However, J.J. didn't come directly in. He leapt up, grabbed the top of the door frame, and chinned himself on it. He held himself up there for a full minute, his biceps swelling, then dropped lightly to the ground. Stephie watched him. Since Matt's death she was seeing all her friends with an unnatural sharpness. She had never before noticed that J.J.'s close-cropped mat of curly blond hair was faintly green from chlorine. He swam in competitions all over the nation and the past year had come close to the Olympic qualifying time. "You guys look gloomy enough," J.J. complained. He hooked his fingers together and stretched his arms over his head. "Who died?" Too late he realized what he had said and his face turned an unbecoming pink.

"Stephie was just saying she couldn't believe the police couldn't find out who was driving Tony Dickson's Ford pickup."

"How do you know they haven't?" said J.J. "Maybe they have a lead they aren't telling us about."

"They asked me some questions that night after the party," said Dennis. "And they came around a few days later, too. I started to feel like a prime suspect. Did they talk to you?"

"You better believe they talked to me. It was my party. I figure they talked to everybody."

Dennis nodded. "Yeah, they wanted to know when I last saw Matt and whether he'd seemed drunk. They kept wanting to know if anybody went out and came back, like I would notice something like that. I mean, it was a party, for pete's sake. People all over the place. I don't think they're ever going to find out what happened. Just another sad example for Mother's Against Drunk Driving. I bet the case is closed."

"I thought they never closed the case on murder," Stephie said. Dead silence followed her remark. Stephie realized she sounded melodramatic and was embarrassed. A soft clunk made her glance toward the doorway. Jordan was coming in and had dropped his umbrella. He knelt to pick the dripping umbrella up off the floor. "It's pouring out there," he said, raising his straight, dark brows.

"We were just talking about what the police are doing about Matt's death," Stephie said.

"But, Stephie," said Dennis, "it had to be an accident. Nobody thinks the poor jerk who hit Matt knew what he was doing."

"Maybe. But he murdered Matt just the same as if he had held a gun to his head."

"We shouldn't be talking like this," muttered J.J.

"The real problem is," said Dennis, "that there were too many people at the party."

"Yeah, you know the way it is," put in J.J. "When you have a party, everybody in the world shows up. I don't even know who all was there."

"What J.J. means," said Jordan, "is that whoever hit Matt might even have left the party before the police got there. That's why it's hopeless to figure out who it was."

"Yeah," said J.J., "and after all, it was an accident. Sure, the guy shouldn't have snatched Tony's truck when he was drunk, but then again Matt shouldn't have passed out cold in the middle of the driveway either."

Dennis touched Stephie's hand. "Hey, you okay?"

"Of course, I'm okay. I'm perfectly fine. I just want some straight answers, that's all."

She felt like asking Jordan how he managed to stay so cool. He had been Matt's closest friend. Then she thought about it and realized that she probably seemed pretty normal, too. She was just as tanned as she had been before Matt died. She still had all the requisite arms and legs. It was only inside that she felt so strange. Suddenly, with almost startling intensity and clarity, she knew she was going to have to bring

Matt's killer to justice. That was the only way she would ever find peace.

By now the rest of the team had showed up. "We really ought to get started earlier," said the librarian, Mrs. Anderson. She dumped a bunch of papers on her desk. "The regional competition is next weekend."

"I had an English paper." Jordan propped his eyelids up with his fingers. "I was up till two."

"I can't help it if I'm late," Melissa said. "I was behind a bus the whole way. Honestly! Tell her, Jordan. I live right on the migratory bus route."

It had surprised Stephie when Melissa and Jordan became a couple. Jordan was smart. The phrase "quick on the uptake" might have been invented for him. Melissa, on the other hand, was all sweetness. A little blond bit of a thing, she was mostly fluff. Stephie had always been puzzled about how Melissa had managed to get on the Quiz Bowl team. Matt's theory was that she had cheated on the qualifying exam.

Mrs. Anderson pulled her cardigan around her thin shoulders. "Now, we can do it, team. We just have to work, work, work—keep one eye on the ball and the other on the road ahead."

"The cross-eyed team," quipped Jordan.

Mrs. Anderson fixed him with a baleful look. Jordan was not one of her favorites. "And we don't have much time, so we're going to have to hop to it. Take your places, people. Hurry." They all slid into chairs next to their buzzers. Mrs. Anderson picked up a sheet of computer paper and started tossing out questions. "What researchers won the Nobel prize for discovering the structure of DNA?"

Stephie's finger jabbed the buzzer. *Buzz.* "Watson and Crick." She was glad to see her reflexes were still okay. She always liked Quiz Bowl practice. Of course, she had particularly liked it when Matt . . . She bit her lip and tried not to think about him.

"In the Protestant Reformation—" began Mrs. Anderson.

Jordan's buzzer went off. "Luther!" he said.

Mrs. Anderson peered at him disapprovingly over the top of her glasses. "Jordan, you are just a little too fast with the buzzer. If you'd listened to the end of the question, you'd have known the question was about Henry the Eighth, not Luther. Remember, at the regionals, they're going to give a double penalty for premature wrong answers."

Jordan shrugged. "I don't think I can stop."

"Jordan's an instinctive player." Rachel Grunning's blue eyes shot an ironic glance at Jordan. "He can't help himself." Rachel was dressed, as usual, completely in black—black turtleneck, black tights, black lace-up shoes, and a short black knit skirt. Stephie couldn't remember exactly when Rachel had gone all black. She vaguely recalled seeing her in a pink turtleneck, once, but the memory was faint. Rachel had been monochromatic for months.

"Well, you have a problem with answering too fast, Jordan. Work on it." Mrs. Anderson picked up the second sheet of the printout. "What did I have for lunch?" Bewildered, she stared at the printout and repeated the question in a puzzled voice.

Stephie smiled. "Green eggs and ham!" The entire team collapsed in laughter.

Mrs. Anderson considered them severely over her glasses. "Would someone please explain to me what is going on here?"

Stephie and J.J. exchanged a glance. "We were sort

of fooling around with the computer a few weeks ago," explained J.J. "We changed a couple of the questions. That's all."

Mrs. Anderson frowned. "Can't you see that if you read the questions ahead of time it defeats the whole purpose of the practice?"

"We didn't read them all," Stephie said. "We changed a couple of questions—just for the fun of it."

"I think I'll lock my practice disks up next time to be sure," said Mrs. Anderson. The bell rang with a shrill burst. All the kids jumped at once and made for the door.

Stephie went out into the hall, leaned against a wall, and giggled helplessly. Green eggs and ham! For a minute there, she realized, a blissful minute, she had actually almost forgotten about Matt.

3

When Stephie arrived at the front entrance of the school the next morning, there was no sign of the custodian, and the only sound she could hear was the spitting of water from a roof gutter as it hit the pavement. It was raining. She pulled open the heavy front door and jogged toward the library, anxious to get out of the gloom of the hallway. Tearing around a corner she nearly ran into Jordan at his locker. "Whoa!" He caught her and swung her around until she was breathless.

"Stop it," she cried. "Jordan! Stop!"

All at once he let go. Under his straight brows, his gray eyes were unfocused, as if his thoughts were far away. It seemed to Stephie that since Matt's death, Jordan had been less sure of himself. The corners of his mouth were a little unsteady, as if he weren't sure whether to laugh or cry. She was touched at this new sign of vulnerability. Jordan's careless self-confidence had always been a major part of his charm. That was what had attracted Matt, she was sure—Jordan had had enough self-confidence for both of them. She remembered how annoyed she had been when she learned later that Jordan had stood by making suggestions the first time Matt had phoned to ask her out. She couldn't believe she had been so petty as to get upset about something like that. She supposed she had been jealous of Jordan's influence on Matt, but what difference did it all make now? They had both lost him.

She knew Matt's death had to have left a major hole in Jordan's life. He and Matt had been going to take a trip to Europe over Christmas break. They had been planning it for months. The idea was for them to bum around the French Riviera while everybody else was stuck at home gorging on fruitcake and visiting with boring relatives. That was the kind of thing Jordan liked—doing something glamorous that was just a little bit quirky and out-of-step. If by some miracle the junior class had gotten together and given bake sales to raise the money to go to Europe together, she was sure Jordan wouldn't have gone. Something everybody was doing lost its appeal for him. He was an intuitive aristocrat. Well, he could go by himself, now, if his parents would let him. But somehow she thought he wouldn't. France wouldn't be much fun without Matt cheering on the sidelines. Jordan needed an audience. "If we keep fooling around," she told him, "we're going to be late for practice."

Jordan made a derisive sound. "You don't listen to old Mrs. Anderson, do you? Heck, she's late as much as anybody." He opened his locker abruptly, and the sound of the banging locker door echoed all the way at the end of the hall. Stephie saw something move in Jordan's locker, and her stomach heaved. It was only Jordan's fake shrunken head. He kept it hung from the top of the locker by a thong. All it was was a carved coconut but it looked like a dark, hairy head with a squashed nose. Its eyes were darker gashes in a dark face. She turned her head away hastily.

"Realistic, isn't it?" His face lit up suddenly in a smile.

Stephie managed a laugh. "Yeah."

Rachel and J.J. came careening around the corner just then. Rachel was wearing a black duster over a long black skirt. Something seemed different about her, but Stephie couldn't figure out what.

"We're on our way to the regionals," crowed J.J. "How can we lose?" He slapped Jordan on the back. "We're hot, man. We're so hot we can't stand ourselves." He shot a sidelong glance at Stephie. "Hey, what's the matter? Stephie looks sick. Have you been showing her your filthy pictures?"

"I think she doesn't like my shrunken head." Jordan touched the coconut to set it swinging. Stephie cringed. She didn't see how he could stand to touch it.

J.J. bent down to get a better look. "I have to admit it looks real."

"Maybe I ought to trade up." Jordan smiled. "Get an authentic one. Anybody know a Borneo exchange student who could get me a head secondhand?"

"I'm surprised at you, Jordan," said J.J. with a leer. "You know the student handbook clearly states that no dismembered bodies will be allowed in lockers."

"Cut it out, you guys," said Rachel. "Can't you see Stephie's getting sick. As a matter of fact, when you start talking about dismembered bodies I don't feel so great myself."

Jordan circled Rachel slowly. "You look different. Did you dye your hair or something?"

"I just touched it up," Rachel said in a distant voice.

"Nice." Jordan's smile was like heat lightning, so quick it seemed almost an illusion. "Very black." To Stephie's relief, he slammed his locker door.

Stephie studied Rachel a moment. Sure enough, her hair, which had always been dark, was now an even, dead black that matched her clothes. Her face was pale, almost white, and her long earrings made of jade beads dangled below the stark black hair. She could have been a member of the Addams family.

Dennis came by at a trot. "You guys are going to be late."

"We're always late." Rachel flipped her hair out of her eyes. "Who cares? It doesn't matter."

"Mrs. Anderson won't like it," J.J. said. "She sure didn't like that stuff about the green eggs and ham, either. No sense of humor—that's her problem."

Jordan frowned. "I wonder where Melissa is."

"Probably stuck behind a bus somewhere," said Rachel.

"Why can't she leave five minutes early? Is that so tough?" asked Jordan. "You'd think she could figure out that was the way to miss the buses."

"Hey, man!" J.J. protested. "I thought you liked Melissa."

"Yeah, but it wasn't her brains that attracted me."

Dennis put a hand on Stephie's shoulder. "You okay?" he asked quietly.

"I'm fine, Dennis. You don't have to act like I'm falling apart. I'm perfectly all right." That wasn't exactly true, thought Stephie. She wasn't going to be all right until she found out who had killed Matt.

Later that day, at lunch, Stephie realized she had left her algebra book in her locker. Glancing down the hall, she decided to take a chance on getting it. No one was supposed to be in the hall without a pass, but now and then it was possible to sneak past the hall monitors.

She hurried down the empty hallway, opened her locker, and jumped back, scared, slamming the door shut. Something had moved in there. She was sure of it. But nothing could be alive inside her locker. She opened the door again, very gingerly. From the shadowy interior of her locker, the dark, distorted face of the coconut head stared back at her. Its temple was splashed with red. Stephie backed away, up against the far wall.

"What's wrong?" Dennis suddenly appeared beside her.

Stephie couldn't quite spit out the words to tell Dennis. Her mouth was dry and her heart was pounding erratically.

Dennis glanced at the open locker. "It's that stupid head of Jordan's. Why would anybody put it in your locker?" When he took the head out, Stephie saw that someone had stuck a penknife in its temple. Red paint had been dripped onto the coconut just where the knife went in.

"Jeez, somebody has murdered the poor bugger." Dennis glanced at her. "Want me to pitch it out?"

She hesitated. "I don't know. Jordan is crazy about that thing."

"A fat lot I care about Jordan." Dennis marched off around the corner. Stephie wasn't sure what he intended to do with the head and to be truthful she didn't much care.

She felt off balance. Why would anybody want to put Jordan's head in her locker? It was as if she had been going along peacefully minding her own business and someone had yelled an obscenity at her. What had been a perfectly okay day suddenly had turned bad. When Dennis came back she was still bracing herself against the wall. It was just a prank, she told herself, but since Matt's gory death she was in no shape to laugh off shrunken heads.

Dennis raised an eyebrow. "Who do you think did it? Jordan?"

Stephie glanced at Jordan's locker. It was unlocked, as usual. Jordan was careless about things like that. "Why would he want to do that to me?"

"Dunno. Have you been mean to him lately?"

"No!"

"Who have you been mean to, then?"

"Nobody!"

Dennis shrugged. "Just a prank, I guess."

"What are you doing out here, by the way?" She gave him a sudden suspicious look.

"Have to make up a test for Mrs. Myers." He smiled lopsidedly and held up a hall pass. "I'm legal, see?"

"Well, I'm not. I'd better get back to the lunchroom." Not that she felt like eating anything, she thought.

"Look here, Stephie, I didn't do this to you. I'm your friend, understand?"

"Sure. I know that."

Dennis's eyes met hers in a steady, friendly gaze. Suddenly she realized who he reminded her of—the funny-looking big dog she had had when she was little. Bozo had had a damp, freckled nose and long, straw-colored hair that was invariably muddy and full of burrs. He wasn't a very glamorous dog, but he had a wonderful disposition and Stephie had used him as a pillow on hot summer days. Dennis had the same goofy smile and kind eyes. She couldn't believe she had actually been suspecting him of putting this thing in her locker. She must be cracking up or something.

She swallowed. "Thanks for pitching that thing for me, Dennis."

"Sure thing."

Stephie decided not to mention the shrunken head to anybody. She didn't even want to think about it. Especially, she didn't want to give the prankster the satisfaction of knowing he had gotten to her.

As the day wore on, however, she felt uneasy, as if all the cells and corpuscles of her body knew something was wrong, even though her mind was busy denying it. When the guy behind her in Spanish dropped his book, she jumped a mile. Then, fifth period, she got called to the office.

Mrs. Mosley, one of the office secretaries, was at the counter when Stephie got there. She was a small woman whose elbows barely reached the countertop. "Sugar, one of the students reported that the tires on your car have been slashed." She pushed her glasses back up on her nose with one finger and squinted at Stephie. "We traced you through your parking sticker. We thought you might want to get the tires fixed before school lets out. Do you have any idea who could have done it?"

"No." Stephie shook her head numbly. "None at all."

"We've never had trouble like this before." Mrs. Mosley glared at her. "You can call a garage from here, if you want. I expect your insurance will pay for it."

Stephie shrank a little into herself, dreading what might come next. First her locker, now her car. Maybe she would be next?

She knew it was crazy to think like that. The shrunken head in her locker was only a joke. As for the tires—some vandal had done it. But a voice inside her head, weaving and dipping inside her deepest consciousness, whispered *danger* and the skin at the back of her neck prickled as if she had felt a blast of cold air.

4

When Stephie caught up with Melissa and Rachel outside in the parking lot after school, they were talking about their trip to the regional competition.

"We're going to be staying in the dorm at McNair College," said Rachel. "I wonder if Benji will be back. Remember Benji from last year?"

"Was he the guy who put straws in his nose?" asked Melissa.

"No! Of course not! You remember Benji, don't you, Stephie? He was studying Buddhism." The corners of Rachel's mouth tucked in, making her look smug. "He told me I had amazing eyes."

Stephie noticed Rachel was wearing the ID bracelet Matt had given her. It didn't even go with the funky clothes she wore these days, so why was she wearing it? What could it possibly mean to her? Another trophy? Stephie wondered. Another boy who thought she had amazing eyes?

27

It was depressing for Stephie to recognize that she was still jealous of Rachel even though Matt and Rachel had broken up ages ago. On his own, Stephie admitted reluctantly to herself, Matt probably would have stuck with Rachel a lot longer. They had been very tight, and it was hard for him to break with anybody. People imagined he was tough, but it was only because of the way he spoke, with his lazy, insolent drawl. Behind his thin facade of macho toughness were major fears. One time he and Stephie had gone to the state zoo together, a huge sprawling place. They had gotten separated and when they got back together Matt was in tears. He had confided to Stephie then that he had a recurring nightmare in which everyone he cared about vanished.

Oh, he probably would have held on to Rachel, all right, but Rachel had pushed him away. She had hurt his pride so badly that whatever had been between them was long over before Stephie and he got together. Now Matt was dead, and there was nothing for Stephie to be jealous of anymore.

Stephie was vaguely aware that Rachel and Melissa were still talking about the upcoming trip. It seemed Mrs. Anderson had told Rachel the Quiz Bowl van was going to leave at four in the morning, which was gruesome, but more or less standard. This time, the girls agreed, they were going to have a say in where they ate along the road. Melissa said she was going to get seriously disgusted if they ate nothing but fast food.

Stephie shrank from mentioning her slashed tires. She instinctively felt that if everyone knew about them, that would make it seem more real. Keeping quiet, she could almost persuade herself that the sense of danger she felt was all in her mind.

Jordan jogged up to them. "Somebody told me your tires got slashed, Stephie. What's going on?"

"No joke, your tires got slashed?" Melissa's eyes widened.

"Marilyn Hayden told me about it," said Jordan. "She works in the office."

"Why didn't you say something? Is it some kind of secret?" Melissa asked.

"Stephie must have a lot more interesting life than we thought." Rachel threw her a sideways glance. "What is it, Stephie? Old boyfriend?"

"I think it's terrible the way nobody is safe anymore," cried Melissa. "It's like when all those houses were broken into right in my neighborhood. We've got a permanent crime wave around here. You ought to notify the police, Stephie."

"Ah"—Jordan lifted his dark brows—"but if it's something personal maybe Stephie doesn't want to go to the police."

"It's probably a waste of time, anyway," said Melissa. "They wouldn't catch them. And don't you tease her, Jordan McGuire."

"I'm not teasing her." Jordan's eyes glistened with mischief. "I'm just saying that whatever she's doing, she'd better stop it. This guy isn't fooling around. Next time it could be something really serious, like copying her homework."

Stephie realized that everyone else was smiling but she couldn't bring herself to share in the joke. She found herself thinking that one of Jordan's less attractive qualities was the way he prodded at people. She remembered watching him play tennis once when he had reduced his partner to tears by doing a comic parody of her serve. He hadn't meant anything by it, she supposed. He was so supremely confident that he just didn't realize what masses of quivering jelly everyone else was inside. Stephie could feel her own insides quivering now. The slashing of her tires was far from funny. It gave her a feeling that was close to panic.

"Hey, Dennis!" Jordan waved at Dennis, who was moving toward his beat-up old Plymouth parked in the corner of the lot. "Did you know Stephie's tires got slashed?"

"Tell the world, will you?" murmured Stephie softly.

Dennis ran over to them, his eyes soft with sympathy. "No kidding. Somebody slashed your tires, Stephie?"

She reluctantly admitted it.

Dennis whistled. "I wonder if there's some kind of connection."

"What do you mean? Connection with what?" asked Melissa.

"Somebody put Jordan's shrunken head in Stephie's locker."

"My head was in your locker?" yelped Jordan. "So that's where it went. What'd you do with it?"

Dennis shrugged. "Pitched it."

"Come on, now!" said Jordan. "Why'd you do that?"

"It was ruined, man," protested Dennis. "Somebody murdered it. Don't look at me." He explained about the red paint and the penknife.

"That is *sick,*" said Jordan.

"You've got enemies, Stephie," said Rachel.

"Would everybody quit acting like it's my fault!"

"Nobody thinks it's your fault," Melissa said.

"I dunno about that." Jordan smiled.

"That's not funny, Jordan," said Melissa. "Any one of us could be next."

Several pairs of eyes uneasily sought their parked cars to assure themselves that their tires were still intact.

"Anyway, the garage I called said my insurance will pay for it," said Stephie.

"Great!" Melissa smiled. "And in a little more than a week we'll be going to regionals, and we're all going to have one terrific time! Aren't we?" She looked at each of them in turn. "Well, guys, aren't we?"

A week from Saturday at four in the morning the East Lake Quiz Bowl team piled in the school van for its twelve-hour trip to the regional competition. Melissa had brought along the AAA guide to restaurants and was checking out some possible breakfast stops by flashlight.

"I feel like last week's fish," moaned Rachel. "Why do we always have to leave so early?"

"Because it's good for our character." Jordan punched Melissa in the ribs and she shrieked. That was Jordan all over, Stephie thought irritably, always moving, poking, teasing. He was restless by nature, the kind of person who'd pull a plant up to see how it was growing. He was like a two-year-old with his simple, innocent egotism. It never occurred to him that other people might not be in the same mood he was. He'd better not touch her, Stephie thought grouchily. She was not a morning person and she might just haul off and wallop him one, which would not be a good start to the trip.

Their luggage had to be strapped to the top of the van, and Stephie cast a glance outside and hoped it wasn't going to rain on her duffel bag. Heavy rain and thunder showers had been predicted for the entire East Coast. She only hoped it would hold off until they arrived.

Sumir had been clever enough to bring along a couple of pillows and a large plastic bag of trail mix, which he shared. Stephie winced as she saw him arranging his things around him on the backseat. She was surprised at how much pain she felt looking at him and knowing he was on the team to fill Matt's place. He had been coming to practice regularly, but he had been so quiet she had hardly noticed him. Like Dennis, he was a bit of an outsider. The two of them hadn't grown up with the others and didn't join in their private jokes. Not that you could tell they were outsiders by looking at them. Sumir had a trace of dark hair on his upper lip, which might have been the beginnings of a mustache, but that was the only exotic thing about him. His black hair was covered by a Chicago Cubs baseball hat, and he was dressed in jeans and a blue cable knit sweater. It was easy for Stephie to believe he had been writing a computer program at J.J.'s party the night Matt died. He claimed to be a Hindu, but she always suspected that computers were his real religion.

Mrs. Anderson clipped earphones to her head and put a cassette of classical music in her tape player. "Everybody buckled in?" she asked. "Good. Then let's go." She drove the van out of the school parking lot.

As soon as Mrs. Anderson wasn't looking, Jordan unbuckled his seat belt and stretched out luxuriously. "Wouldn't it be great if we could go to nationals this year?"

"You mean *win?*" said Dennis. "You're forgetting

we only made it to regionals by the skin of our teeth. You're dreaming, man."

"Yeah," Jordan drawled as his glance skated around the van, "but if we could make it into the college computers and get the questions, we'd have an edge."

"I've never understood how people break into strange computers," said Melissa. "Could somebody break into my computer at home?"

"Not unless it has a modem," said Sumir.

"He means it has to be connected to a telephone hookup or something else that connects it with other computers," explained Dennis.

"Oh," said Melissa blankly. "I think I've got one of those things. I've never used it."

"Sure, you have," said Rachel impatiently. "Remember a couple of years ago when we all did that committee report on Russia for world history?"

"We were burning up the wires," said Jordan. "Remember, we were right up against a deadline, but then Miss Collins gave us an extension."

"Yeah, I remember. It came in handy then," said Melissa. "But you mean, I could even get into things like NASA's computer or the school computer?"

"Probably," said Sumir.

Maybe Sumir could, Stephie thought, but the idea of Melissa doing it was a joke. It had been all she could do to send a message to Stephie's computer when they were working on that report. Rachel had had to help her, if Stephie remembered right.

"It might not be so easy to break in," Dennis pointed out. "These big systems are protected with passwords."

"It's not that hard," said Sumir. "Lots of times you can guess them. For example, the most popular password in the United States is *love.*"

33

"No kidding." Melissa looked interested.

"Following as a close second is *sex.*"

Jordan grinned. "Aw right!"

"In England, however," Sumir went on, "the most popular password is *Fred.*"

There was a long silence. "The English must be extremely weird," said Melissa. "So you're telling me we could just break into the McNair College computer and get all the Quiz Bowl questions?"

"Yes, but it would be wrong." Sumir folded his arms and regarded his teammates with his calm, dark eyes.

"Well, sure it'd be wrong," said Rachel, "if you want to get technical about it."

Talking about breaking into the college computer made Stephie uncomfortable. "Knowing the questions would take all the fun out of it!"

"Besides," Jordan made a cutting motion across his throat with his index finger, "if we got caught we would go directly to jail and would not collect two hundred dollars. That would sure look great on our permanent record, wouldn't it?"

Stephie blinked. Jordan thinking ahead—she never thought she'd live to see it. Maybe they all were growing up, after all. Certainly she felt older. It was Matt's death. It had made her realize that everything doesn't necessarily turn out all right. Maybe it had hit Jordan, too. She had always felt she could see in the spoiled, pettish set of his mouth, the look of a guy who had been given a Corvette when he turned sixteen and imagined that life was only an endless succession of pleasures that were his for the taking. That illusion must have been hard to hold on to when his best friend was crushed under the wheels of a truck. She swallowed as the horrible image of blood on the pavement rose in her mind. Matt's dying had been an end to so many things.

Stephie jumped as Dennis touched her temple gently. He smiled when her startled eyes met his. "Hey, you've got a curl right there. That's nice." He smiled at her again with his slightly goofy expression.

Dennis hadn't actually asked her out, but Stephie was sure enough of him to be wondering if she would go. The real problem was she couldn't be at all sure how she felt about Dennis, her mind was so full of Matt still. Whenever Dennis spoke, she found herself thinking that his voice wasn't low and sexy like Matt's. Instead, it was light with a little break in it as if he were surprised by life. He blinked a lot and his eyes shifted as he talked. Matt had been different. Matt's eyes bored so deep into hers that it seemed he could see her soul. She shivered. It was crazy to go on continually comparing them like this. She was never going to be able to appreciate Dennis for who he was as long as Matt filled her head.

Stephie wondered again if Jordan thought of Matt all the time. They had been so close—the star and his audience, A and B, two sides of a coin. Each had been so necessary to the other that Jordan must feel Matt's loss as a perpetual ache. Did Jordan have bitter regrets the way she did? Matt and Jordan had quarreled that last night. She knew Matt had begun resenting him since Matt had become obsessed with being independent. He was trying to break away from him. He was trying to break away from her, too, it seemed. Look at the way he had struck out when she tried to get him to stop drinking. She could understand now what had been going on with him, but that night at J.J.'s party all she could see was that he was embarrassing her. The last words she had screamed at him were angry.

That still haunted her. Did some hasty last words ring in Jordan's ears, too? Jordan had a quicksilver surface that created the illusion that he was above being hurt. If he got the horrors the way she did when he woke up at two A.M. and stared at the ceiling and thought of Matt's blood spattered all over the pavement, it didn't show.

As the van tooled along the highway toward McNair, the sun came up and the team tried to decide where to stop for breakfast. Stephie leaned back against the seat and glanced around her. Jordan's face, with its characteristic straight nose and straight dark brows was profiled against the fluff of Melissa's hair. She was snuggled up against his shoulder, head bent, flipping through the AAA guide. "This place called Sandy's doesn't sound too bad," she said.

"Just so long as it has something besides danishes," said J.J. "I need a real breakfast."

"Breakfast is the most important meal of the day," said Melissa sagely.

Jordan groaned.

"Well, it is! Studies show that. I forget just why but it's perfectly scientific." Melissa looked around defensively. "Probably something about carbo-whatcha-macallits or carbo-whatevers. Anyway, carbo-some-thing."

"Or something." Jordan grinned. "Melissa, it's a good thing you're cute because you ain't no rocket scientist."

"I'm okay if you don't throw a whole bunch of syllables at me all at once."

"Or the nine multiplication tables," put in Rachel.

"That's different. I made a conscious decision not to learn the nine tables. It's a waste of time. I *could* learn them anytime I wanted, but I don't need to since they invented calculators."

Sumir looked pained and shifted his position restlessly. "Hey, Jordan, somebody told me you just got tickets to Lollapalooza. How'd you do that? I heard on the radio they were all sold out."

"Jordan's dad's got connections," said J.J. "He could only get two, though. We're going to drive down that Friday and spend the night. That way we don't have to fight the traffic."

"We got backstage passes, too," Jordan put in. "We get to touch those guys, man."

Rachel nudged Melissa. "You ought to go along with them, Melissa."

"But I hate heavy metal music."

"Yeah, but you could visit your sister at State while the guys go to the concert."

Jordan was obviously annoyed. "Want to straighten my collar for me next, Rachel?"

It was provoking, Stephie thought, the way Rachel always tried to arrange everybody's life. Jordan had pulled those tickets out of a hat purely to cement his relationship with J.J., and the last thing he wanted was Melissa tagging along. He was digging hard, trying to fill the hole left in his life by Matt's death, she thought.

"I don't want to visit my sister," protested Melissa. "I'd be talked to death. She's got these three boys on the string and none of them knows about the other. Two of them are named Matt and one is named Nat, but so she can tell them apart she calls one Hat. Not to his face, of course. But, like, if her roommate says 'Who was that who called just now?' she'll say 'Hat' because otherwise it's too confusing." Melissa giggled.

"Anyway, her life has gotten super complicated and all she does is talk about it."

"Matt, Hat, and Nat? That's not a life," said Jordan. "That's a line from a limerick."

Melissa laughed. "I tell her she's going to get them mixed up and call one of them by the wrong name someday but she says no problem because they'd never even notice the difference. As long as she doesn't start going with somebody named Bryan, she says, she's in safe city."

That Melissa's sister had two boyfriends named Matt seemed nightmarish to Stephie. She pressed her fingers against her temples. *Matt, Matt, Matt*—the name buzzed in her brain.

"Jeez, I wish it weren't so far to McNair." Sumir stifled a yawn. The conversation languished. Rachel, half-asleep, leaned her head against a window. In the overcast, early-morning light everyone looked gray, as if they were all suffering from a lingering illness. A vague feeling of dread hung over Stephie. Matt, Matt, Matt—she couldn't stop thinking about him. "Does anybody else feel like there's a ghost with us?" she burst out. She studied each of them defiantly.

Dennis recoiled as if she had struck him.

Melissa peeked around Jordan. "You mean Matt?"

"For me, Matt is eternal," cried Rachel dramatically.

"What's that supposed to mean?" snapped Jordan.

Rachel placed her palm over her breastbone and gazed soulfully. "I keep him here, in my heart."

Stephie felt a sudden desire to hit Rachel over the head with Sumir's bag of trail mix.

"Do we have to get morbid?" asked Jordan. "When are we going to stop talking about this, huh?"

"I guess I'll stop when I find out exactly what happened," said Stephie.

"You really want to know who was driving that truck?" Dennis shook his head. "I'm not sure that I do."

She heard Dennis's light, pleasant voice ringing in her ears and realized he couldn't possibly understand how she felt. He was reasonable by nature, while she was filled with black grief and a rage that practically choked her. It wasn't Dennis's fault that he was basically too nice a guy to see where she was coming from. It was as if he were painted in pastels and she in black and red.

"Yes, I really want to know who did it." Stephie spit the words out. "I'd like to see the rat put in jail."

"Give it up, Stephie," advised Dennis softly. "It's hopeless."

"I doubt if the police have really tried to find him." She bit her lip.

"What can you do that the police couldn't do?" asked Jordan.

"I'm not sure yet." She hesitated. "But I'll think of something. I know a lot of kids, and I was there the night it happened. I wouldn't be surprised if when I start trying to fit things together I come up with something. Have we ever really tried to reconstruct exactly what happened that night? For instance, what was Matt doing outside? When I think about it, it's very peculiar. Usually I had to drag him away from a party. Don't you remember how he was always the last one to leave?"

"Stephie Yates, Private Eye." Jordan smiled.

For once Stephie didn't rise to the bait. Let Jordan tease her. She didn't care. If she found out who had killed Matt and made sure his killer got charged with vehicular homicide that was all she wanted. Maybe she had been right when she said there was a ghost among them. Maybe Matt's memory or his ghost, whatever one called it, was refusing to let her rest until she brought that drunk driver to justice.

The murderer regarded Stephie through dangerously narrowed eyes. Her problem was she didn't know enough to back off. She needed a lesson. It would be awfully convenient if she would disappear, like through a trapdoor. Too bad it didn't work that way. If Stephie was going to disappear, somebody was going to have to help her along. But that shouldn't be hard for somebody who happened to be a minor genius at improvisation. There was bound to be some way or other to get at her without anybody knowing. Right?

5

Stephie tossed her duffel bag on a chair in the dorm room. She had been riding in the van so long everything she had on felt dirty. She got clothes out of her bag and pulled on a fresh pair of jeans. After she sprayed a little cologne behind her ears she felt a hundred percent better. Too bad Rachel wasn't changing, too. Stephie was sort of curious to see if Rachel's underwear was black. And what about her dental floss? If they made black dental floss, she was willing to bet Rachel would have it.

Rachel threw herself down on her bed. Lying there still and pale in the dim light, she looked even more like Morticia than usual. It was so spooky that Stephie felt compelled to switch on a lamp.

"I hope Melissa can get some quarters," Rachel said. "You've got to have change for the vending machines around here. Not that Melissa cares about the change. She was just looking for an excuse to go off

with Jordan—she's absolutely obsessed with him."
Rachel rolled over and caught Stephie in her blue-eyed gaze. "Tell me the truth, Stephie, don't you think
Jordan is incredibly immature and self-centered?"

"Oh, I don't know." Stephie shifted her position
uncomfortably and wondered what Rachel was getting at.

Rachel's eyes widened. "He's got an infantile personality disorder. Truly. I've been reading up on it."

Stephie gazed at her friend in sudden amusement.
Where did Rachel come up with the strange facts she
did? One time she had persuaded them all that they
ought to test their dishes at home for lead content.
Rachel was so sure they were all being poisoned that
Stephie had actually started thinking she could feel
herself growing weak from lead poisoning. She had
even begun to imagine her vision blurring and was
positively astonished when all the dishes in their
kitchen tested lead-free. Sometimes Stephie wondered if those weird blue eyes of Rachel's had hypnotic powers. She remembered how stupid she had felt
doing scratch tests on all her mom's dishes, and she
told herself she was going to be careful not to fall
under Rachel's spell again.

"Seriously," said Rachel earnestly, "haven't you
noticed how he's simply *got* to have his own way?"

"I like to have my own way, too. So does everybody."

"Well, sure. But with Jordan it's sick. I mean, why
do you think he hooks up with these pathetic clinging
types like Melissa? If she ever had an independent
thought, he'd freak out. I'm not kidding. He has to
have people *tied* to him. It's like he can't stand it that
they're separate people with their own lives. He thinks
Jordan McGuire's the most important person in the

world and if anybody crosses him he becomes *enraged*. I've tried to warn Melissa about him, but she won't listen."

I guess not, thought Stephie. She probably thinks you're trying to put her off Jordan so you can have him yourself. Still, Stephie could see there was a touch of truth in what Rachel was saying. Jordan was used to having his own way. He was the baby of his family, and his three brothers were already grown. Jordan always seemed able to go to the city for any concert or ball game he wanted. She had never heard him say he had to be in early because it was a school night. And then there was the Corvette. Not your average sixteenth birthday present. Stephie didn't know if she could call him spoiled, exactly, but chances were he hadn't had much practice at being disappointed.

"You remember that I used to go with Jordan." Rachel spread her fingers and studied her blue-veined hands thoughtfully. "Back in the seventh grade."

Stephie could not understand what boys found attractive about Rachel. Between her boniness and the way she lectured people, Stephie thought any boy would be thoroughly turned off.

"I remember Jordan's folks took him to a fair," Rachel went on, "and he got a couple of buttons, you know, like campaign buttons? Only you could have any message you wanted printed on them. He got one that said Jordan Loves Rachel and he got another one for me—Rachel Loves Jordan. Well, I wasn't going to wear it! I mean, even in the seventh grade I had a certain sense of style. So I told him I lost mine. He got so mad he took his off and stomped on it! I'm not kidding you. He ground it under his heel right there on the school sidewalk!"

Stephie knew Jordan would hate Rachel's telling

that story on him. She figured if anybody could have driven him to distraction, it would have to be Rachel, and she couldn't quite hide the smile that flitted across her face.

"You may think that was funny," Rachel snapped, "but listen to this. When I broke up with him, he started shaking me until I bit my tongue. I could taste the blood. He said, 'Nobody breaks up with me.' I was scared stiff."

Stephie glanced at her curiously. "You never mentioned this before."

"I guess I felt funny about it. As if it were my fault or something." Rachel's blue eyes held Stephie's. "Well, you can see why I don't want Melissa to get involved with him, can't you?"

"But, Rachel, that was in the seventh grade! That was years ago. We've all grown up a bit since then, haven't we? I mean, I hope. I wouldn't want anybody to hold anything I did back then against me!"

Rachel turned her face away and the lamplight shone on the flat, unreal black of her hair splayed out on the pillow. "You just don't believe that Jordan is bad for Melissa, do you?"

It occurred to Stephie once again that Rachel was jealous. Maybe she was finding out she didn't like to watch Melissa zipping along in Jordan's Corvette, drawing all the admiring looks. Stephie reached for an emery board and carefully repaired a jagged bit on her thumbnail. "I just think Melissa can take care of herself, that's all."

"Hah!" Rachel sniffed. She might have said more, but just then Melissa bounced into the room.

"I've got a lifetime supply of quarters, guys. If I fell in a river I'd sink like a stone."

"Great!" Rachel sat up and flashed a fake smile. "I

guess I'll get a shower now." Stephie watched as Rachel shed black garments all the way to the bathroom until she was down to black satin underpants. Her back was so bony Stephie could count the vertebrae. The bathroom door closed behind her and a second later the shower came on.

"Can you believe that?" Stephie tossed the emery board to the bed. "Black satin underwear?"

"Rachel always was one to go overboard. Remember when she died her hair purple?"

"I know, but at least that washed out. I think she's carrying this black thing to a ridiculous extreme even for her. What's she trying to prove?"

"I thought you knew, Stephie." Melissa looked at her soberly. "It's because of Matt."

"No! It can't be. It's been going on longer than that! Months even. And she was wearing black the night of the party. I remember!"

Melissa nodded. "Yup, that's right. She's been wearing black ever since she and Matt broke up."

The notion that Rachel was wearing permanent mourning for Matt hit Stephie like a physical blow and it took her a minute before she could think clearly. "It doesn't make any sense," she said at last, standing and pacing. "Why should Rachel be wearing black for Matt? It was her fault that they broke up in the first place. Matt told me. He said his mother sent him to the mall to get something and there was Rachel in the ice-cream shop making out with Chad Hendricks!"

Melissa nodded. "I know, but the thing with Chad was sort of a wild impulse. She never really wanted to break it off with Matt. She says she realized after they broke up that he was the only boy she ever really loved."

"Oh, come on!"

Melissa looked at her reproachfully. "You ought to be nicer to her, Stephie. It's been really tough for her since Matt died."

"She always wants to be the center of attention. That's her trouble," Stephie said bitterly.

"You don't know what she's feeling," said Melissa. "Nobody knows what other people are really feeling. Like, I happen to know that she tried to make up with him the very night he died!"

"You mean at the party?"

"That's right."

"But—"

"We could hear you yelling at him. We could all tell you were breaking up. Rachel probably thought it was a good time to go back with him."

Stephie sat down suddenly on her bed. She knew she needed to take in what Melissa had to say. No matter how unpleasant it was, she had to find out about the events of the night Matt had died if she intended to find Matt's killer. Just then a distant rumble of thunder sounded and the lamp flickered.

"Hey!" yelled Rachel from the bathroom.

"I hope the lights aren't going off," cried Melissa.

That was all they needed. As if they didn't have enough of a horror-house atmosphere with Rachel mooning around in heavy mourning. Stephie checked the lamp, but the bulb seemed to be in tight. She hoped McNair College didn't have one of those unreliable electrical systems that shorted out at the first drop of rain. "We'll just have a blackout party if the lights go out. No big deal."

"No big deal!" Melissa blinked rapidly. "We could b-break our necks. Have you seen this place? Stairs everywhere. And we don't know where anything is!"

"Well, don't fall apart. It's not even dark yet."

"It will be pretty soon." Melissa glanced anxiously out the window.

"The lights aren't going out, Melissa!" Stephie took a deep breath. "Okay, so you were saying Rachel tried to make up with Matt. That's what you were telling me, right? What happened next?"

"I think he was real nasty to her. He was real nasty to everybody." Melissa looked away from Stephie and carefully pleated the bedspread with her fingers. "He was mean." She flushed. "He was ever so sweetsie to you and a couple of other kids, that you didn't see him the way I did. Sometimes I just plain hated him."

Stephie could almost hear Matt saying, "Melissa makes Malibu Barbie look like an intellectual." For the first time she wondered if Matt had ever been tactless and said that in Melissa's hearing. "A cloud of hair with a glomming instinct," he had called her. Too bad she couldn't ask Melissa about it.

"Not that I wanted him to die or anything!" Melissa went on quickly. "I was really sorry. I mean, it was awful. But there's no use pretending he was nice just because he's dead. Did you know he told Jordan he wouldn't go to France with him? He knew Jordan's folks wouldn't let him go by himself so he decided to pull out just to spoil it for Jordan. I heard him say so."

"He was drunk."

"That's no excuse."

"No." Sadness crept into Stephie's voice. "No, I know it's not." She didn't think she could make Melissa understand that Matt lashed out only because deep inside he cared too much about what people thought of him.

"He was a power freak." Melissa's hands had unconsciously balled into fists. "Think about it,

47

Stephie. He always had this thing about power. He thought Jordan had all this control over people, on account of his being so popular and good-looking and all, and so he had to be right next to Jordan. He was sort of like Jordan's first lieutenant. And you know how Rachel can get people to do things."

Stephie laughed. "I was just thinking about that, actually."

"She's incredible. Remember in eighth grade when she got everybody to follow her off the playground into the woods?"

"Looking for Indian arrowheads."

"I got poison ivy and had to miss being in the school play. Well, Matt loved it that she could do that kind of thing. Get people to do things, you know. That was the way he wanted to be—a Pied Piper. I always figured that was why he liked Rachel. He was always mean to me because he figured I didn't rate. Nobody does anything I say, that's for sure. Not even my dog."

"Am I supposed to be some secret power freak, too?" asked Stephie. She could hear the slight edge in her voice. "Is that why Matt went out with me?"

"I think he really liked you, Stephie. I'm not saying he didn't. But think about it. You have an awful lot of determination once you get your mind set on something. It was like Matt was trying to suck all that stuff out of other people. Like those extraterrestrial creatures and flying saucers and stuff that when they're visiting earth they suck all the juice out of power lines."

"Extraterrestrial creatures, right." When Melissa talked the sense got so mixed in with the nonsense sometimes it made even the sensible things she had to say sound a little silly.

"Sure. You know how when a flying saucer lands,

everybody's radio blanks out and the car ignition won't work? Well, Matt was like that. He wanted to be strong so he just attached himself to strong people."

"It's an interesting theory," Stephie said bleakly. "But how do you explain that he was blowing everybody off the night he died?"

"He was a jerk." Melissa darted a sudden anxious glance at Stephie. "No, really, Stephie. He was. Maybe he finally decided he was such hot stuff he didn't need you or anybody else."

Stephie didn't argue with Melissa because she sensed there was a grain of truth in what she had said. True, Melissa had put everything about Matt in the most unsympathetic light possible, but it was hard denying that he did treat people badly sometimes. He had treated her badly. That was why they had had such a big fight the night he died. What it came down to, she decided, was that he hated who he was. He was trying desperately to fit some impossible romantic image of what a guy was supposed to be. Maybe that was really what Melissa had meant when she said he was a "power freak."

6

Later, when the girls went to the cafeteria for dinner, Stephie became aware of the distant thunder again. The weather's menacing mood suited hers. All she needed to finish it off were three witches crying "double, double, toil and trouble." In a pinch Rachel could fill in for one of the witches. All the same, Stephie hoped it wouldn't rain just yet. She glanced up at the sky. The clouds were like black smoke in the twilight.

"I didn't even bring a raincoat," whimpered Melissa. "And look! It's going to pour."

"A little rain won't kill you," said Rachel.

Melissa sniffed and hunched her shoulders as if she were bracing herself for a deluge.

"Besides it may not start for hours." Lightning flashed again and again against the dark sky but the air was cool and still. The storm must not be too close. As they walked to the cafeteria the conversation dragged. Stephie was still trying to digest what Melissa had said about Matt—Melissa who was so seldom openly critical of anyone. Stephie hadn't realized how much she had disliked him. But she couldn't believe Melissa had hated him enough to murder him. No! It was impossible.

Stephie had convinced herself that *someone* had killed Matt, though. But who?

She wasn't certain where she should begin. She had one idea—to make a timetable to check people's alibis, but unfortunately there had been a mob of people at that party. It was going to be hard to sort out what happened.

The cafeteria was hot and crowded. There was a good bit of noise, an acrid smell of burned grease, and lots of kids walking around in sweatshirts printed with the names of their schools. Stephie spotted Mrs. Anderson over by the condiments table with a bunch of teachers. Then she saw the guys madly waving their arms at them. They made their way over to join them.

"You could have saved yourself the trouble of going through the line," said Dennis, glancing at Stephie's tray. "The food's terrible. We're going for pizza as soon as we figure out where to go."

"Where's J.J.?" Stephie asked.

"He couldn't eat this slop. I think he went to get a candy bar." Jordan smiled. "I'm happy to announce, folks, that J.J. and me have already tried to get into the college computer. Turns out there's a terminal in the lounge of the dorm."

"I didn't notice it," said Melissa, impressed. "What happened?"

"Well," said Jordan, "first we tried to get in using the password *love*. No dice."

"*Sex,* same story," put in Dennis.

"I could have told you that," Stephie said. "A college computer's not going to use dumb passwords like that."

"That's what he thought. So we used our heads." Jordan tapped his forehead. "We tried *guest.*"

The obviousness took Stephie's breath away. Naturally, a big computer would have to have some generic sort of password for people who just used it occasionally, visiting professors, for example. *Guest* was just what somebody with no imagination would use.

"And we got in," said Jordan.

Stephie leaned forward in her chair. Suddenly she remembered that what they had done was very possibly illegal. It was certainly unsporting. Self-consciously she leaned back again. "You shouldn't have done that."

"You guys with moral scruples will be glad to know we couldn't find the Quiz Bowl questions." Jordan's eyes sparkled. "We gave it the order to search and tried *Quiz Bowl* and *questions* and the date of the competition and for good measure we tried *guest* again. No luck."

Sumir was interested in spite of himself. "Did you try—" He stopped in midsentence, guiltily.

"It's lucky you didn't get in," said Stephie. "We'd have had to disqualify ourselves, wouldn't we?" No one said anything. She looked around the table at them. "Well, wouldn't we?"

"Sure," came a chorus of voices. She stared at her friends unhappily. Nobody but Sumir seemed very worried about the morality of peeking at the Quiz Bowl questions. And nobody seemed to be interested in bringing Matt's killer to justice, either. What was wrong with them? Or did she have it all backward? Was she the one who was getting strange? She imagined her yearbook picture captioned "Crusader for justice and truth" and flushed a little.

"Look here," said Dennis. "We got a schedule of the matches." He pulled a much-creased handout sheet from his jeans pocket. A grand parade was first thing in the morning, and the competitions were afterward.

"I think we've got a chance," said Dennis.

"A snowball's chance," said Jordan.

Stephie noticed that Melissa was whispering something to Rachel right then. Her gaze crossed Stephie's briefly. Could they be talking about her? Stephie felt self-conscious. She supposed they were saying she was a goodie-goodie. Maybe they were right.

"I said, what do you think?" Dennis repeated patiently.

"What?" Stephie blinked at him.

"Are you asleep or something?" he asked. "Maybe the food is drugged." He prodded his meat loaf with a fork. "Tell me, do you think it smells like bitter almonds?"

"You really know how to cheer a guy up, don't you?" complained Jordan. "I already ate some of mine. I'm starting to feel sick."

Dennis gave Stephie's arm a friendly squeeze. "Hey, you look dead." He seemed really concerned about her, and once again she was struck by Dennis's deep-down niceness. On the Quiz Bowl team, a hotbed of prickly egos, Dennis was steady and solid. She couldn't see him as part of the undercurrent of uneasiness at the table that was setting her on edge. He was separate from all that. She looked around at the rest of them quickly and it seemed everyone's eyes shifted away as if they were avoiding her glance.

Suddenly she remembered that she had gotten up at 3:00 A.M. No wonder she was getting paranoid. "I'm going to the dorm." Stephie pushed her chair back and got up. "I need sleep more than I need food."

"We'll bring you some pizza," promised Dennis.

Outside the cafeteria the cool air wiped the uneasiness from Stephie's mind. College kids in sweaters and jean jackets were trudging toward the cafeteria and student union. It was almost nightfall and she could barely make out the dorms against the backdrop of hills and dark skies. As she watched, lights came on along the walkway. Suddenly she saw J.J.'s red windbreaker ahead of her. When he walked under a lamppost, she could just make out the texture of his curly blond hair. It was J.J. all right with that contrasting band of blue that ran along the sleeves and shoulders of his red jacket. Besides, not too many people had his swimmer's build with those very broad shoulders and narrow hips. He was mounting the steps that went up the hill to the dorms when suddenly a little, thin guy in a baseball cap came charging up the steps past him. In his headlong charge he knocked up against J.J. What came next happened so quickly that Stephie could scarcely believe her eyes. J.J. gave the guy a hard push that knocked him off his feet. The smaller boy fell, bumped down a few steps and sat there looking up incredulously. He yelled something that Stephie didn't quite catch, but J.J. didn't even look back. He trotted lightly up the steps and was gone.

Stephie stood stock-still on the sidewalk. She couldn't believe J.J. had pushed somebody so much smaller than he was. In fact, it wasn't like J.J. to lose his temper period.

Wait a minute, she told herself abruptly. There's a simple explanation for this. The fellow in the red windbreaker can't be J.J. It's that easy. There must be heaps of powerfully built guys with red jackets and curly blond hair in a whole college. Absolute heaps of them.

But as she walked toward the dorms she found uncomfortable ideas insinuating themselves into her mind. Maybe she didn't really know her friends as well as she thought. She knew their favorite rock groups and who they went with. How much did she really know about what was going on inside their heads, though? For all she knew J.J. could be one of those split personalities or have a secret life of some sort. She was always hearing surprising things about people. "No, I don't believe it!" was a pretty standard response to gossip. Like when she had heard the rumor that her geometry teacher was secretly dating a student. Who had told her that? Probably Matt. He was a world-class gossip. He loved knowing what was going on with other people. She remembered how furious he had gotten when she teased him and told him he'd grow up to be a gossip columnist.

She pulled the drawstring of her hood tight until only her nose was peeking out. She wanted to draw back inside it like an animal burrowing and hibernating for the winter. Things were going on that she didn't understand and she was frightened.

She was glad when she got back to the dorm and snuggled up under the covers. She felt safe there, alone in her narrow bed. Soon she drifted off into unconsciousness.

Stephie was dreaming that she was walking down a long corridor but couldn't find her classroom. She had signed up for a course, but had forgotten to go all semester. Now it was time for finals and she couldn't find the room. She was lost, frantic—then suddenly the entire world rocked. "Wake up!" cried Melissa.

When Stephie opened her eyes Melissa was there bouncing on her bed. "The boys are bringing over pizza."

Stephie wasn't sure how long she had slept. It was still dark, but rain beat monotonously on the dorm windows now. The lamp flickered then burned brightly once more, shedding its light on the bed in a broad yellow semicircle.

Rachel pulled her up. "Let's go. I have dibs on the pepperoni."

"I can't believe they went out in all this," said Melissa. "The pizza's going to be sopping wet."

"Oh, come on," said Rachel. "They only had to go as far as the student union."

Bleary-eyed with sleep, Stephie struggled out of bed and let Melissa and Rachel lead her out to wait for the guys. They were going to their room to eat. The dorm had an outside staircase that mounted to the second floor where a broad landing formed a kind of porch. The single light overhead shed a feeble glow on the cement surface. Standing on the landing, the girls thought they'd be protected from the downpour but flumes of spray blew in on them with every change of the wind and Stephie's jeans soon began to feel cold and clammy. "Why are we waiting out here in the rain? Let's go back inside," Stephie said.

"They ought to be back any second," said Rachel. "And we said we'd wait here."

"Watch that railing, Stephie," Melissa cautioned. "Don't lean on it. It may not be strong. Also it's not very high."

Out on the sidewalk the rain made crystal haloes around the tall lights.

"There they are!" cried Rachel, waving.

Stephie could see the guys as they trotted under the

lights, their bodies hunched protectively over the pizza boxes. J.J. had his red windbreaker wrapped around his head turban style, white bags of drinks dangling from both hands. Rachel and Melissa cheered as the guys reached the steps, running.

"Slow down," yelled Melissa. "The steps are wet, guys. You're going to slip."

"I want pepperoni," cried Rachel.

By this time the boys were on the landing, too. It was pretty crowded. "Give me my drink," said Melissa, reaching toward J.J.

"Hang on," said Jordan. "Wait till we get inside."

"I just don't want somebody else to get all the pepperoni," said Rachel.

Just then they were plunged into darkness. The lights went out. The blackness around Stephie felt profound. It was velvety deep and wet.

"I knew it!" Melissa broke into sobs.

"Oh, shut up," snapped Jordan, and Melissa's sobs subsided as suddenly as they had begun.

The entire campus was black, and Stephie could make out only a few distant blurs of headlights on the main road. The wind blew rain against her face as she felt the reassuring pressure of the aluminum railing against her thigh. Then suddenly, she felt someone shove her in the middle of her back, and the aluminum railing bit into her thigh with bone-bruising pain. Then, to her horror, she was falling over the railing into the inky darkness. A scream tore from her throat.

7

When Stephie next became conscious, she heard a siren wailing above her head and was aware that she was speeding along in a vehicle. "I think she's coming to," a strange voice said. Her head ached and when she put her hand up to her forehead, it felt wet. She opened her eyes and saw that her hand was a red and white smudge. Everything was blurred. She sat up suddenly. "I can't see!"

"That's a common effect of head injuries," said a male voice. "Don't worry."

Stephie felt a hand trembling on her shoulder. She turned and saw that Melissa's face was blurred. "Just lie down," Melissa said in a quavering voice. "You're going to be fine. We're on our way to the hospital in an ambulance."

Stephie was soaking wet. Her knee hurt, her jeans were sticking to her, and her sweatshirt was muddy, and that wasn't all. Blood was streaming down her face. She wondered if she was dying, like Matt. She closed her eyes, not wanting to see how odd everything looked. She was sure her skull was fractured. Panic fluttered inside her.

"You're okay. It's going to be all right," said Melissa. "We're almost there."

"What happened?" gasped Stephie.

"The lights went out for a minute and you fell off the landing," said Melissa.

Stephie felt confused. Something was wrong. She touched her wet face again.

The ambulance attendants strapped Stephie to a stretcher, rolled her out of the ambulance, moving swiftly through the rain. They bumped her up a curb. A light on the portico of the building said Emergency. She was relieved that she could make out the word even though between the rain and her blurred vision the sign looked as if it were smeared clumsily onto the darkness. The cold stung her face. Blood, she thought. I've got blood all over me. Big glass doors slid back automatically and she was rolled into the heat and light of the hospital. She seemed to lie in a white room a long time while stretchers were wheeled past her and people were coming and going. Everyone was too busy to bother about her. She closed her eyes and felt as if she were floating in pink darkness. "X-ray for you, young lady," said a brisk voice finally.

No fracture, was the verdict of the X-ray technician. The doctor's diagnosis was a concussion. As soon as Stephie heard that, she began to feel better. The aching of her head was no longer ominous, and even the blood on her sweatshirt and the pain in her knee seemed more bearable. Someone slit her jeans up one leg, wrapped an Ace bandage around her wrenched knee and advised her to take it easy. It seemed she was going to live. Suddenly she wanted to be dry. Dry socks, dry underwear, dry sweatshirt would be blissful.

Mrs. Anderson and Rachel were waiting for her with Melissa when she was wheeled back into the examining room. Under the fluorescent lights, Mrs. Anderson's skin looked bluish. Her hands were fluttering anxiously about her face.

"I don't think we're going to have to keep her overnight," said the doctor. "As long as someone can sit up with her and keep her awake until morning. If she blacks out again or starts seeing double, you need to give us a call."

"We can take turns staying up with her," said Rachel. "Nobody sleeps when we're at competitions anyway."

Mrs. A. didn't bother to protest that her team members needed a good eight hours bed rest. She looked too demoralized to lay down the law about anything. "We're going to have to call your mother," she told Stephie.

"Well, don't scare her to death," Stephie said. "I'm okay." She really would have preferred that her mother know nothing about what had happened. She didn't want to add to her mom's worries, particularly when there was nothing she could do. Stephie gingerly touched her wet hair, glad there were no mirrors around. She knew she must look awful. Her forehead was bandaged, but no one had taken the time to clean her up, and she could feel the dry blood puckering the skin on her face.

"Can you walk?" asked Melissa.

Stephie slid cautiously off the gurney and stood up.

Her right knee felt unreliable when she took her first hobbling step.

Mrs. Anderson hastily put an arm around her and Melissa supported her on the other side. "Take it easy," said Melissa.

"I'm fine," Stephie insisted. "Really."

Rachel took the keys and ran ahead to the van. Mrs. Anderson held a big black umbrella over Stephie, and the three of them stumbled awkwardly to the van in the parking lot.

Stephie was bundled into the middle seat of the van. "It was so unfortunate, the lights going out like that." Mrs. Anderson turned on the ignition and drove the van cautiously out of the parking lot. "One of the teachers was telling me that the college is trying to get the town to modernize its electric facilities, but in my opinion they shouldn't wait for that. They ought to have a backup generator. It's a matter of safety. I just hate to face your mother, Stephie, if—well, I'm not going to think about it. It's just too awful. We can be thankful it was no worse. What a dreadful accident!"

"It wasn't an accident," Stephie said. "Somebody pushed me."

Up in the front seat, Mrs. Anderson and Rachel exchanged a quick glance. They didn't say anything and Stephie decided they thought she was delirious. She had to admit, now that she said it out loud, that the idea of someone's pushing her seemed absurd.

"Don't be silly, Stephie," said Melissa from beside her on the seat. "It was an accident."

Melissa's words sounded like an unfortunate echo in Stephie's throbbing head. Matt had had an "accident," too. She hugged herself and shivered.

"They told us," said Rachel, "that you probably

wouldn't remember what happened just before you fell. Besides, you were half-asleep."

"That's it!" said Melissa. "You're getting it mixed up with a dream. You weren't really awake when it happened."

"I know that somebody pushed me," Stephie said stubbornly. "I could feel two hands planted right in the middle of my back."

"There was a lot of confusion," said Rachel. "Probably somebody bumped up against you without realizing it."

Nobody could have bumped against me like that, Stephie thought. It was impossible. But she didn't say anything.

"Why would anybody want to push you off that landing?" asked Melissa. "You could have been killed."

When she put it that way, Stephie couldn't think of a reason. Melissa was right. This wasn't a joke, the way the head in the locker and the tires might have been. Stephie felt a vein throbbing in her temple and cautiously put a hand to her bandage. To her relief it didn't appear to be leaking fresh blood.

"You'd better not get excited," said Rachel. "Just take it easy."

"How is your head, Stephie?" asked Mrs. Anderson anxiously.

"It hurts," she admitted. Her hands and elbows were burning, too, where they had gotten skinned. Obviously she had instinctively put out her arms to save herself.

"They said you could take aspirin," said Mrs. Anderson.

"I've got some in my suitcase," said Melissa. "Is everybody going to be glad to see you! I called the guys from the hospital to let them know you were okay. The last time they saw you, you were being loaded into an ambulance, dripping blood. It was really a shock." She giggled nervously. "You know, we heard you scream but at first nobody could figure out what had happened. People kept saying, 'What was that?' 'Who screamed?' You know how confusing it is in the dark. But then the lights went on and there you were down on the ground sort of crumpled up in a puddle of water."

"I just about had a heart attack," cried Rachel. "I mean, I'm still getting this terrible shortness of breath whenever I think about it. It was horrible!"

"It wasn't that great for me, either," Stephie pointed out.

"Yes, but you were *unconscious*," countered Rachel. "You were feeling no pain. It was the rest of us who were going through hell. J.J. ran to get Mrs. A. and somebody went in to call the ambulance. The blood running off you was turning the puddle you landed in pink." She shuddered deliciously.

"The boys wanted to get you out of the rain, but I said we shouldn't move you," said Melissa, "in case your neck was broken or something."

"We were *sure* you were dead," said Rachel.

Stephie felt it was indecent of Rachel to be enjoying herself so much.

"No, no. That's not true," Melissa said. "I didn't think you were dead. I could tell you were breathing and then the ambulance got there super fast. They must have been nearby."

"Stephie, I want you to go slow tonight," Mrs. Anderson warned. "No running around the dorm. Understand?"

The idea of her running all over the dorm was

laughable, thought Stephie. She ached all over. She wasn't even looking forward to walking up the stairs to her room. Even though she couldn't actually remember falling, she had a kind of low-grade, sickening fear huddling inside her stomach ready to burst out whenever she thought of going back to the dorm.

"Melissa, Rachel, remember that you can't leave Stephie alone. If you feel as if you can't stay up, you must come get me so I can sit up with her."

"We'll take good care of her," promised Rachel.

Her tone sounded ironic, but when Rachel smiled sweetly back at her, Stephie told herself her imagination was running away with her. Her head throbbed and the lights of the street sped by outside the van coloring the rivulets of water as they slid down the windows. She felt almost dizzy. Maybe Rachel was right and she had gotten dreams and reality mixed up. Her head hurt when she tried to remember the actual event, and finally she sagged thankfully back against the cushions of the van and thought of nothing at all. She only wanted to melt into the darkness.

"Stephie, don't close your eyes!" said Mrs. Anderson sharply. "Keep an eye on her back there, Melissa."

Stephie opened her eyes and stared out the side window into the blackness. It was going to be a long night.

8

Stephie felt so disassociated from what she was doing that it was almost as if she were watching herself in a film. It was rough going up the stairs with her aching knee, but she managed by bracing herself against the railing.

"Come on, Stephie," said Melissa. "Are you okay?"

"I'm fine," Stephie said at once. She knew she was attracting curious stares as she limped down the second floor hall. "I just want to get into some dry clothes." She touched the bandage on her forehead gingerly. The cut on her forehead was not deep, she realized. The emergency room hadn't thought it even needed stitching up. But it hurt. And her forehead and cheek felt as if they had been scraped across grit.

"The boys have gone to get doughnuts." Melissa bent to read a note taped to their door. "Sumir is the only one who stayed behind."

Stephie went into the bathroom and stripped. She

was very careful pulling her sweatshirt over her head. Her skull was throbbing. Once she had her clothes off, she patted herself dry, then put on a shirt and baggy jeans. Her knee was too swollen for her to get into her tight black jeans, the only other pair she had with her.

She did the best she could with her sodden, tangled hair, considering that she couldn't bring herself to brush it. Facing the bathroom mirror finally, she went rigid. In spite of the bandage like a white gash across her forehead, she looked like Matt. The tousled dark hair, the shadowed eyes were his. She stared at the mirror in horror.

Melissa threw the bathroom door open and Stephie jumped. "Why don't we go down to the guys' room?" said Melissa. "We can wait for them there."

"Yeah, uh, sure," stuttered Stephie. The important thing was not to be alone, she told herself. Her imagination did strange things when she was by herself. She was beginning to believe that the someone who had murdered Matt was trying to kill her now. Even Melissa's smile seemed sinister.

Stephie limped along behind Melissa and Rachel as they went to the other side of the dorm where the boys' room was. When no one answered the girls' knock, they pushed the door open and were met by a blast of music. Sumir was sitting on the bed in the dark. Stephie noticed a spiral of smoke curling up from a shallow cup of incense beside him, which explained why the air was pierced with a strange sweetness. He leapt up and switched on a lamp. "Are you okay, Stephie?" His dark eyes searched her face, but what he saw must not have reassured him because his gaze shifted.

"I guess I'm okay." Stephie sank into a chair at once. "Nothing's broken, anyway."

"Are you warm enough?" Sumir pulled the paisley bedspread off the bed and draped it over her legs. "We didn't even realize you were missing until the lights went on and Melissa spotted you down there on the ground. I thought maybe the railing had given way, but then I saw it hadn't. What did happen?"

Stephie started to shake her head and then thought better of it. "I'm not exactly sure."

"They told us she probably wouldn't remember anything that happened just before she fell," Rachel put in. "The concussion does that."

Stephie wondered if the person who had pushed her had been counting on that. But he was out of luck. She remembered enough to know she had been pushed. Or maybe he had been counting on her ending up dead. But why did anybody have any reason to kill her?

"It's weird." Sumir's dark eyes were puzzled. "The floor of the landing wasn't really that wet, was it? Not wet enough to be slippery. I just can't figure it out. The railing is low, but it looked to me like you'd really have to lose your balance in a major way to go over like that. Did you trip on something?"

"It just goes to show we should have been more careful," put in Rachel.

"You're right," said Melissa. "We should have stayed in place and held hands when the lights went out."

"Oh, come on," said Rachel. "We can't go around holding hands every time the lights go out."

"Look what happened when we didn't," said Melissa.

"Doughnuts!" Dennis burst in the door followed by Jordan and J.J. "Hey, how about some more light in here?"

Stephie blinked as the overhead light went on.

"Gosh, Stephie"—Dennis knelt down beside her—"you look awful."

"Thank you." Stephie pulled the bedspread up under her chin and glared at him, vaguely resentful.

"Are you okay?" His eyes were anxious.

"I have a concussion and my knee's pretty messed up, but I am expected to survive."

"Couldn't they wash you up a little better?" Jordan made a face. "You look like you came fresh from the guillotine."

"Oh!" Stephie's hand flew to her face. "I thought I had gotten all the blood off."

"Great comment, Jordan," said Rachel. "Very compassionate of you, I must say."

"I'll get you a washcloth," said Dennis, leaping up.

"We've got blueberry filled, lemon filled, or powdered." Jordan flipped the doughnut box open.

"Stephie ought to get first choice," J.J. said. Stephie turned to him. She thought he was a bit pale—and then suddenly she recalled what had happened after dinner that night. That boy he pushed down the stairs! It seemed like years ago but it had only been a matter of hours. She shot J.J. another uneasy glance as she helped herself to one lemon filled and one blueberry. The hollowness of her stomach reminded her that she hadn't really eaten since lunch. After what had just happened to her, her theory that the boy in the red windbreaker hadn't been J.J. seemed pretty weak. How many guys were built like J.J.? Not many.

Jordan held out the box to J.J., but he shook his head. "I think I'd better give them a miss."

"In training?" Jordan smacked his lips loudly. "Too bad. Guess I'll have to take your share." He hooked a doughnut and bit into it, showering powdered sugar all over the floor.

Stephie thought it was odd that J.J. was passing up calories. She wondered what had made him lose his appetite so suddenly. Normally, he was one of those guys who thought nothing of eating two huge stacks of pancakes smothered in butter and syrup. He was acting strange, all right. Just glancing at him now she could see that something was the matter. His face definitely was white and strained.

Dennis came back with a warm washcloth and a hand mirror and gazed at Stephie with concern while she dabbed at her face to get the rest of the blood off. Fresh from the guillotine? She shuddered. Jordan's remark reminded her of what a close call she had had.

Sumir turned his tape over and the music started up again.

"What's that you're playing?" asked Jordan.

"The Grateful Dead."

"I went to a Dead concert once," said Melissa.

"I've been to five," said Sumir. "One of them we sat on a hillside under the stars. I wish I'd lived in the sixties. Back then people didn't spend all their time worrying about their SAT scores like we do now. They just figured anything goes."

Stephie had seen the sixties on television—riots and girls boogying in short flowered dresses. Woodstock. Kent State. It looked to her as if things had been completely out of control. Right now what appealed to her was law and order.

Melissa bit into a doughnut, got blueberry jelly on her chin, and wiped it off with the back of her hand. "I can't see you with a flower behind your ear, Sumir."

"You'd get used to it." Sumir shrugged. "What I hate about the way things are now is you can't get away from competition. It's like it saturates everything you think or do. That's the nineties for you. You can't afford to foul up. You've always got to be thinking about how things are going to look on that college application."

"You're right about that." Jordan lowered his dark level brows. "One little mistake can mess up your life for good."

J.J. seemed uncomfortable. "Nothing's that big a deal—you just do the best you can and then don't worry about it."

"Easy for you to say," said Sumir. "You've got the grades, and you're practically Olympic material besides. All the best schools will be after you. But with me, until I got on Quiz Bowl, I didn't have anything to put down that looked good. I read a lot and fool around with computers, but on paper I look like nothing."

It was odd to realize that Sumir must have been glad when Matt died. As first alternate, he had automatically got moved onto the Quiz Bowl team. At last he had an impressive extracurricular activity to put down on his college applications. And he was good at Quiz Bowl, too, Stephie admitted to herself. He had the kind of precise mind that accumulates a lot of information. She had already learned that on sports questions he was unbeatable. And he was better than Matt on every subject because half the time Matt couldn't keep his mind on the game.

"Well, I'm not worried about getting into college," said Melissa. "I want to go to East Carolina like my sister, and I can get into there pretty much no matter what. I'm a legacy."

School wasn't a big thing in Melissa's life, Stephie thought, her gaze resting on Melissa's heart-shaped face. It was Jordan Melissa cared about. Melissa had only succeeded in getting Jordan's attention after she made Quiz Bowl, but Stephie happened to know she'd been interested in him for a long time before that. Maybe it wasn't fair to call it an obsession, the way Rachel had, but there was no denying Melissa had a thing for him.

What would have happened if Matt had proved that Melissa had cheated on the Quiz Bowl exam? She would have been kicked off the team. Would Jordan have dropped her? He might have. The story would have got all over school and people would have thought it was funny—ditzy Melissa cheating so she could tag along after Jordan. Jordan wouldn't like it. He didn't care for stories that made him look ridiculous.

Stephie had to admit he did have the knack of inspiring devotion. It wasn't just Melissa. Matt had looked up to him, too. Melissa had been right about that. Sometimes Stephie had resented it. Looking back, she knew she had been more than a little jealous of the closeness the two boys had shared. Maybe that was why she had gone off Jordan lately.

"Matt would have laughed to see us talking like this!" said Rachel.

"Don't start, Rachel!" warned Jordan.

"Start what?" She glared at him.

"You know what. Carrying on. Acting a big tragedy to make yourself look important."

They eyed each other with open hostility.

"I only meant," Rachel said coldly, "that Matt didn't believe in worrying about college applications. He didn't plan to go to college anyway. He was going to do something really neat with his life, like be a poet or a race car driver."

"How would you know?" said Jordan. "You and Matt weren't even speaking. Hadn't been for months."

Rachel stood up, her eyes blazing. "That's because our feelings ran too deep for words. What we had together was something more profound and spiritual than anything you could understand, Jordan McGuire. We knew *everything* about each other."

"Maybe Matt didn't like what he knew about you," suggested Jordan.

Rachel slapped Jordan's face. Then she stepped back and gasped, obviously frightened of what she had done.

Jordan's breathing quickened but he didn't speak or move.

"Honestly," Melissa cried. "Do we have to be like this? Can't we just be friends?"

Rachel cast a contemptuous glance at Melissa before turning and stalking out of the room.

"So we have Rachel being Rachel." Jordan's voice was a bit unsteady. The red print of Rachel's hand was visible on his cheek.

"You did that on purpose," said J.J. with a reproachful glance at Jordan. "Didn't you?"

Jordan laughed. "Okay, I admit it. I've about had it with Rachel's official widow bit. At least now we don't have to hear her go on and on about Matt until we all feel sick to our stomachs."

Helpless tears were streaming down Melissa's face but she didn't try to defend Rachel.

"It's been a rough day." Sumir shot an uneasy glance around the room. "I guess we're all kind of coming unglued."

Stephie was relieved when Sumir turned up the volume and switched off the lights so they could barely make out one another's faces. She knew the others must be sneaking glances at her, wondering about her reaction to Rachel's outburst, but the truth was she couldn't bring herself to care right then about anything Rachel did or said.

The heavy sweet smell of the incense gave the darkness a strangely ominous flavor, and the pulse of the music began to feel to Stephie like her own heartbeat.

"Don't close your eyes, Stephie!" cried Melissa. "Stephie's not supposed to go to sleep, you guys."

Stephie's eyes opened wide and she tried to make out the faces of her friends, pale blurs in the dim light. Which one of them hated her? she wondered. Which one of them wanted to kill her? She put her hand to her throbbing head. No, she had to quit thinking like that. Nobody wanted to kill her. It was because her head hurt that she was thinking like that, suspecting everybody.

"You're not going to be able to play tomorrow, Stephie," said Dennis. "Hey, Sumir, could you turn that thing down some. I can't hear myself think."

Melissa sniffled and wiped her nose. "You better just sleep through the grand parade in the morning, Stephie. Then you can come and watch part of the competition if you feel up to it."

"I'll come and watch the parade." Stephie didn't like the idea of being alone in the dorm.

"Oh, no. You'd better get some sleep," insisted Melissa.

Stephie didn't argue.

As the night wore on the conversation turned to the meaning of life, and Stephie found it hard to follow what people were saying. Her eyes were open but she was so tired she was weaving in and out of consciousness. "If you don't believe in Adam and Eve," Melissa said earnestly at one point, "you've got a real problem." Stephie was totally surprised and realized she hadn't heard whatever had preceded this odd statement. Her eyes were open, but most of the time her brain was asleep. She wasn't sure of what anyone said during the rest of the night.

When day was breaking, she and Melissa went back to their room. Stephie could hear the shower running. Rachel must be getting ready to put on fresh black clothes. Really, it was irritating, Stephie thought wearily. Things were bad enough without Rachel pitching fits.

The windows were already becoming bright squares of morning light, so Melissa pulled the venetian blinds closed. Without another coherent thought, Stephie dropped into her bed and fell asleep.

9

When at last Stephie woke up there was no sign of either Rachel or Melissa and the small dorm where only the Quiz Bowl participants were staying was strangely quiet. The light through the venetian blinds painted stripes on the wall and on her arm and watch that said 10:30. Rachel's black clothes were heaped in a sordid bundle near the bathroom door. It was so quiet it was creepy. If only she could have heard one ordinary innocent sound like water running. But all around her was only ominous silence. Stephie lay there a moment listening to her heart thump. She was all alone, she realized. Everyone else had gone on to the competition. She groped for the schedule on the bedside table. A quick glance at it told her that the parade was long over and the matches must be underway. She jumped up out of bed, suddenly sure that she didn't want to be alone in that huge empty dormitory. She no longer felt woozy. Her mind was perfectly clear, and the one thought that was in it was that somebody had pushed her off that landing.

She struggled into her baggy pair of jeans, grabbed the schedule of events, and limped off to the auditorium. East Lake was scheduled to be in the auditorium at ten. She found the auditorium with no problem and as soon as she went in, she saw her teammates lined up behind buzzers onstage. They were facing off against some team from Georgia and at the moment Sumir was calmly listing the stages of cell division. Only a scattering of spectators were sitting in the auditorium. Spotting J.J.'s curly head, she sat beside him in the last row.

"Hi." She stole an uncertain look at him. "What's going on?"

"I'm sitting this one out," he said. "Taking my break while I can."

Now that she wasn't playing, Stephie realized, the team only had one extra player and her teammates' breaks would be few and far between. "Maybe I could play the next match."

"Nah, don't worry about it. No sense killing yourself." J.J. clasped his hands and stretched his arms. "We're going to lose anyway."

"Pessimistic, aren't you?"

"Realistic." He glanced at her. "Stephie, do you ever feel you aren't sure who you are, anymore?"

Stephie thought of the moment the night before when she had had the strange sensation she looked like Matt. "Sort of," she said uneasily. "I mean, I understand what you're saying."

"Sometimes something just comes along and grabs you." J.J. socked a fist into his palm. "Your life is out of control, you know? And there's nothing you can do about it." He turned away and for a long while didn't say anything. She wondered if he had forgotten she was there.

"It's like my life is over," he went on quietly. "Like I'm not me anymore, like something else has taken me over and there's nothing I can do about it. It's like I'm a zombie."

Stephie shrank from him. "J.J., what exactly are you saying? What are you trying to tell me?"

"Huh?" He cracked his knuckles and met her gaze. "Nothing really. I guess I'm just spouting off."

"It's never too late to turn your life around, you know," she said quickly. She felt she had to say something hopeful. "There are, uh, doctors and things. Therapy and stuff. Nobody's beyond hope."

"That's what you think," he muttered. He suddenly stood up and the seat snapped back against the chair's back.

"Where are you going?" Stephie was alarmed.

"Out." He thrust his hands in his pockets. "Maybe I'll jog some—I guess."

Stephie wondered if she should go with him. Perhaps she should, but she couldn't. When J.J. flexed his muscles like that and began talking about being a zombie, she was afraid.

He had only been gone a moment when Dennis suddenly plopped down beside her. "I thought it looked like you out here," he said, obviously pleased.

Stephie glanced up at the stage and saw that people were leaving. The match was over and she hadn't even noticed. "Don't you have to be at the next match?" she asked.

"This is my break time. It's J.J.'s turn to fill in for me."

"I hope he makes it back in time. He left here a minute ago and said he was going jogging."

"Well, that's his problem. I'm finished for now. So, how are you feeling? You're looking a lot better."

Dennis looked kind, Stephie thought, which, in a lot of ways, was better than looking good. She wondered why she hadn't thought before of confiding in him. He was relatively new in town. His dad had been transferred in by some big company from Idaho or Utah or something, which made him the logical one to talk to. There was no way he could be involved in what had happened that night. She was sure he didn't know Matt well enough yet to hate him, and she knew he had only been drinking apple juice at the party. He couldn't have been the one who pushed her off the landing, either. He *liked* her. That was very relevant. And he had those wonderful, soft, caring eyes, rimmed with pale lashes, that made her feel she could trust him. She desperately needed someone she could trust.

"Are you okay, Stephie? You seem awfully quiet."

She lifted her chin slightly. "Well, I'm not doing so badly considering somebody pushed me off that landing."

"Wait a minute, didn't you fall because you were still half-asleep from your nap?" Dennis was acutely uncomfortable. "With concussions, you know, a person can get mixed up."

"I know, that's what Rachel said, too. She claims I was half-asleep and that I dreamed someone pushed me. But that's not true. I had had a nap, but I wasn't dreaming about being pushed or falling. I was dreaming about corridors and classrooms and stuff like that."

"I've had that dream. You've got a class but you don't know where it is?"

"Yes, that was it. When Rachel and Melissa came and woke me up and we went outside, I woke up right away from the rain blowing on me. So I wasn't asleep."

"If you say so."

Stephie knew he didn't believe her, and really, when she thought about it she could see why. Maybe she wouldn't have believed it either if she hadn't felt those hands in the middle of her back. "Well, it happened," she insisted.

He blushed. "But why would anybody want to hurt you? They'd have to be out of their mind."

"Maybe somebody knows that I'll never give up until I find out who killed Matt." She gritted her teeth. "And they're right—I won't. I want to figure out who did it more than ever because what this tells me is that Matt's death wasn't accidental." Belatedly, she cast a cautious look around but she saw no sign of the other kids. "The problem is I don't know who I can count on anymore. Just now J.J. was telling me he's a zombie and his life is over."

"No kidding!" Dennis lifted an eyebrow. "What do you think that means?"

"I don't know, but I hope to find out. I'm going to try to find out a lot of things."

"But, look, Stephie, if you really believe somebody killed Matt, aren't you taking a big chance asking a bunch of nosy questions?"

"Naturally I'm not telling anybody that I'm doing detective work."

"Good. Because you don't really know that anything is wrong, do you?"

"I felt somebody push me," Stephie reminded him.

"Right," he said hastily.

"Hasn't it occurred to you that there are a lot of things you can't know about other people? I mean, sure, they all seem pretty sane and all, but what you can't know is what it would take to make them snap."

"I guess what you're saying is that everybody has a breaking point?"

Stephie nodded.

"People are on edge," he admitted. "I can see that. Like Rachel slapping Jordan last night."

"That's the kind of thing I mean!"

"Yeah, but it's a long way from slapping somebody to killing somebody."

"The basic idea's the same," insisted Stephie. "Everybody's got a breaking point. Everybody. And after you've killed once it must be easier to do it again."

"You really think that's what's going on?" he asked dubiously.

"Look at it this way. First somebody kills Matt and then somebody pushes me off the landing. There *has* to be a connection."

Dennis frowned. "I just thought of something. How would anybody even know it was you? It was pitch-black. You couldn't see a thing."

"I didn't move after the lights went out. And I did say something. You could tell where I was by where my voice was coming from."

"Besides," Dennis said, "I'm sure I could tell you if I came up against you in the dark. You have this particular smell, you know? That perfume you wear."

"Ma Griffe. It's cologne. Ever since it happened, I keep looking around and wondering who it was who pushed me. Somebody has cracked all right. I just don't know who. And believe me when J.J. starts saying he's a zombie, I get chills."

"You think J.J. did it?"

"Well, something is bothering him." Stephie described the incident she had seen after supper.

"That doesn't sound like J.J. Are you sure you got it right?"

"I couldn't exactly see his face."

"It might not have been him, then."

"But he was built like J.J. and dressed like J.J. If it looks like a duck and quacks like a duck . . . Honestly, Dennis, it's so creepy. I've known J.J. for years and all of a sudden I can't trust him anymore."

"Well, you can trust me, Stephie."

She impulsively squeezed his hand.

"I'll tell you what, though," he said, "I'll bet this turns out to be an accident after all. I just can't believe anybody would push you off that landing. You could have been killed! It just doesn't make sense for somebody to murder Matt, either. Heck, if people started knocking off all the obnoxious guys at East Lake High, hey—" He grinned.

"You may be right." Stephie withdrew her hand from his.

"But you don't believe me."

"No."

"And you're going to keep poking around to see what you can find out."

"Yes."

Dennis heaved a sigh. "Well, for heaven's sake, watch yourself, will you?"

Stephie scarcely knew what she did the rest of the day. She more or less functioned in a daze. She consulted the printed schedule and followed her team around watching them play, of course, but she couldn't have sworn to the details. She was busy turning the events of the past number of weeks over in her mind, trying to make sense of them.

When the competition wound to a close that afternoon, East Lake wasn't even in the top twenty, but no one's spirits seemed dampened by the loss. When they all went back to the dorm people were telling jokes and singing stupid songs, as usual. Stephie did not join in.

I can't go on like this, she told herself as she stuffed her sweatshirt into her duffel bag. I can't go on half-suspecting everyone, wondering what happened and being afraid. I've got to find out the truth. Dennis might not really believe that there was a murderer among them, but he hadn't felt those hands planted in the middle of her back.

It was dangerous to go after a murderer, Stephie reminded herself, but it was more dangerous not to. After all, he had tried to get her once. He was probably only waiting to get at her again.

During the long trip home in the van the next day, most of the kids fell asleep, but the murderer, sitting at the back of the van wide-awake, watched Stephie. Her dark hair had fallen over the white bandage on her forehead. Her mouth was partly open and she was breathing with the heavy, regular rhythm of sleep. She was a rather pretty girl even with her mouth open, and she didn't look like an avenging angel. Or a detective either. Maybe it hadn't been necessary to put a scare into her. Maybe that was overreacting a little. But it had been like a gift when the lights had gone out like that. No time to think, and too good to pass up, really.

10

Stephie figured she would go at her investigating just the way she would attack a school assignment. She'd start out by getting an overview. Monday, as soon as they got home, she went to the library to check the newspaper accounts of Matt's death. When she laid the front page out before her, she knew at once why her mother had hidden the papers from her. Directly under the headline was a grainy picture of a police officer standing over a white sheet. The bottom of her stomach seemed to fall out as she stared at it, and images of Matt sped through her mind. She could see him running a comb through his hair, his dark eyes glittering slits the way they were when he laughed. Like a sharp pain she remembered him bending close and warm to kiss her.

There was no use thinking of that now. Setting her jaw, she spread the newspapers out on the long library table and read the newspaper account. Unfortunately, it told her little she didn't already know. It did put the time of death at midnight, however. If the newspaper was right, no more than fifteen or twenty minutes had passed between when she last saw Matt and when he had died. That was the crucial fifteen or twenty minutes. She checked the papers for the next two weeks just in case the police had reported any new developments, but she came up cold. The story had shrunk from two columns on the first day to a mere two inches weeks later. The police had no leads.

The door of the library swung open and a rush of cold air stirred the newspapers as Jordan and J.J. came in. Galvanized, she stood up, wheeled around suddenly and moved quickly to the paperback rack. She stood there, pretending to study *Ten Days to a Better Memory* until Jordan tapped her on the shoulder.

She turned, hoping she managed to act surprised to see him.

J.J. scowled. "Catch those papers spread out all over that table. People are such slobs. I guess they don't want to leave room for anybody else to work, huh?"

Stephie felt her smile grow stiff. The last thing she wanted was for J.J. to take it into his head to tidy up the newspapers. He'd know then that she had been reading the accounts of Matt's death and was bound to wonder why. "What are you guys here for?" she asked quickly.

"Research paper for American history." Jordan made a face.

"Me, too," said J.J. "I should have been working on mine for the past two weeks, but I just didn't get down to it." He ruefully hoisted a stack of books. "Overdue. And I haven't even got started."

"I'm just about in the same shape," said Stephie. "But I can't seem to concentrate. I'll have to come back tomorrow."

J.J. placed his overdue books down on the circulation counter and began counting out the money for fines. Jordan moved toward the library table with the newspapers, idly smoothing his dark hair with his palm.

"Matt used to do that," Stephie said suddenly, stopping him.

Jordan blanched. "What?"

She made the sweeping motion with her hand. "He picked up all your gestures. Remember?"

"I wish you wouldn't hit me with that kind of thing all of a sudden."

"You want me to pretend Matt never existed?"

"Yeah," Jordan said bluntly. "I do." He started to raise his hand to his hair, then stopped self-consciously and hooked his thumbs firmly in his belt loops. "The other night I was watching 'Wacky World of Comedy' on TV and I started thinking, Gee, Matt would love this. I swear I was halfway to the phone before it hit me that he was gone." He took a deep breath. "Give me a break, Stephie. I don't need it."

She bit her lip. She realized she was so caught up in her own feelings she hadn't been worrying much about what Jordan might be feeling. "I'm sorry. You're right." She turned and left the library quickly, without glancing back. It was bad luck that the guys had come in while she still had all those newspapers spread out on the library table but to gather them up and hide them now would only call attention to what she had been doing. She wished she'd been able to hide the front-page story, the one with the big police photograph right under the headline. All she could hope was that they were too worried about their American history papers to pay any attention to a heap of newspapers.

She opened her car door and slowly slid in behind the wheel. Her knee was still stiff and swollen, which made getting in the car painful. Only six other people had been on that landing when she fell, she reminded herself as she backed out of the parking place. J.J., Jordan, Sumir, Rachel, Melissa, and, of course, Dennis. Unless she had somehow imagined the whole thing, one of them had pushed her. It would be better for her if they all thought she had given up on the idea of finding Matt's killer. If the murderer guessed she was on his trail he might take desperate action—but she couldn't keep thinking about that or her courage would give way.

She turned the car toward Melissa's neighborhood. The newspaper photo of Matt's body reminded her that Melissa had been taking pictures the night Matt died. Flashbulbs had been popping in people's eyes all night. Suddenly Stephie wanted to see those photographs. She could almost hear Melissa's little-girl voice explaining that her camera had its own clock. It stamped the time the picture was taken on each frame. If she could only get her hands on those pictures, they might tell her a lot about what had happened on the night of the party. They might even tell her who had an alibi and who didn't.

While she was trying to sort out the facts, she vowed she wouldn't do anything stupid, like stand near a precipice with one of the suspects. In fact, the less she was around them all the better. Not that she really suspected Melissa. Or Dennis. That would be carrying suspicion to a ridiculous extreme. But she was going to be careful not to be alone with any of the others.

Melissa lived in a plush subdivision called Mallowwood. Her big white house was set well back from the road on a hill, which made it look even bigger. In front of it was a substantial stretch of hardwood trees unlike the ordinary lawns of houses in more modest neighborhoods. It must be nice, Stephie thought, to have money. At Stephie's house, money had been a problem ever since her parents' divorce. Her mom had recently been forced to take a promotion to territorial saleswoman, which meant she only got home weekends. It wasn't ideal, but it was the only way they could possibly meet the mortgage payment. Even with that extra money coming in, it wasn't easy.

Stephie climbed two flights of steps up to the front door and rang the doorbell. The bell chimes sounded faintly as if they were somewhere in the next county.

Melissa seemed vague when she came to the door, but her eyes came into focus when she recognized Stephie. "Stephie! Come on in."

Melissa's bedroom could have passed for the control room of the starship *Enterprise*. It was full of electrical things with dials and red and green lights, some of which blinked. Stephie noted a computer, a television, a digital clock, and a compact disk player plus a few other things with dials that she didn't recognize. For all she knew Melissa had Geiger counters or even slot machines in there. A bunch of frayed schoolbooks, heaped on her streamlined desk seemed out of place amid the high-tech toys.

"I've been thinking about that new camera of yours," Stephie began.

"Are you thinking of getting one?" Melissa brightened. "They're terrific. Want to see some of my pictures?"

Stephie was relieved that the first hurdle had been gotten over so easily. "I'd love to," she said honestly.

Melissa picked a yellow envelope off her desk and dumped out a thick stack of snapshots. She leafed through some before handing the stack to Stephie. "I wish I had taken my camera to regionals, but I keep forgetting that I have it. So far, this is all I've got."

Melissa's snapshots never would have made the pages of *Modern Photography.* First came a shot of the seat of somebody's jeans, very close up so you could see the top stitching. Then came a shot of what looked like a blank wall.

Melissa peered at them over Stephie's shoulder. "At first it kept going off accidentally—till I figured out how it worked. So then I took a bunch of pictures at J.J.'s party. That was when I finally caught on to what all the buttons were for. Most of them anyway."

Stephie paused at a shot of Dennis stretching his mouth into a clown smile with both pinkies.

"Some people get real self-conscious if you turn a camera on them," said Melissa. "I saw this great documentary on channel four about this family in Mongolia and the photographer said he lived in their yurt night and day for a month and took pictures of everything until they quit paying attention to him. Then he could get natural shots. That's what I wanted to do, but people kept complaining about the flash. Do you think the guy in Mongolia didn't use a flash?"

"Could be." Stephie flipped to the next snapshot and winced. It was of her and Matt just after they had arrived. Seeing the camera, Matt had suddenly crushed Stephie to him in a big bear hug until she could feel the buttons of his shirt pressed into her cheek so the back of her head was all that showed in the photograph. Matt smiled broadly over her head, his dark hair falling carelessly in his face. His smile gave no sign whatever that that would be the last night of his life.

Melissa gently took the stack of photos away from her. "You don't want to look at these, Stephie. I'm sorry. I forgot."

"I do want to look at them!" Stephie cried. "Really."

"They'll just make you sad."

"No! I want to see them!" Stephie said desperately. "In fact, can I borrow them for a while?"

"Why? When you go to the camera store, they'll show you some sample photos that are a lot better than mine. I'm a klutz with the camera."

"Well, I'm not really thinking of getting a camera," Stephie admitted.

"But I thought you said—"

"I really want to try to figure out what happened that night, Melissa. You see, you've got a sort of documentary record of it in these photos."

Melissa stiffened. "You're getting *morbid* about this. I wish you'd just let it drop. The way you keep bringing it up isn't doing anybody any good."

"Don't you see that with the times stamped on these pictures, they might even give people alibis?"

"What do you mean 'alibis'?" Melissa said sharply. "We're not talking about murder. What happened to Matt was an accident."

"Maybe. But then again maybe not."

"You are getting truly weird, Stephie." Melissa's voice was shrill. "Excuse me but I don't think we should talk about this anymore."

"Don't you want to make Matt's killer pay for what he did?"

"No," said Melissa. "I don't. And you don't have to

look at me that way, either. I feel sorry for whoever hit Matt. I do! If they had the least idea what happened, it must have been horrible. I figure they've already paid enough. You'd better quit talking about it. Take my advice, it's not healthy."

Stephie's hand moved involuntarily to the bandage on her forehead. Was Melissa threatening her? No, Stephie decided when she took in Melissa's wide innocent eyes. She couldn't have realized the way her words sounded. Maybe she was right. Maybe trying to find out who killed Matt was not such a good idea. But Stephie had to do it anyway. She knew she would never have any peace if she walked away from it now. She wished she hadn't been quite so open with Melissa about why she wanted the photos. She hadn't expected such a violent reaction.

"I've got a lot of homework," said Melissa coldly.

Stephie pulled on her jacket. "You aren't mad at me, are you?"

"Stop this, Stephie! You're not going to bring Matt back—no matter what you do. I don't mean to be nasty or anything, but you are getting truly strange. I'm only telling you for your own good!"

Stephie did her best to act suitably chastened.

"I think you'd better go now." Melissa pointedly turned her back on Stephie and pushed open the bedroom door.

The minute Melissa's back was turned, Stephie snatched the yellow envelope of photographs and stashed it under her coat.

"Okay." Stephie smiled brightly. "Maybe you're right. I better be getting on home."

Melissa stood there, irresolute, her hand on the doorknob. "Honestly, the best thing to do is forget it.

It really is." It was obvious that she wasn't really comfortable with the way she had spoken to Stephie.

To make sure the envelope wouldn't fall out from under her coat before she got to the door, Stephie squeezed her arm tightly against it to hold it in place. "I've got to work on an American history paper, anyway."

Melissa cleared her throat. "By the way, how's your head?"

Stephie started to touch her bandage again but remembered just in time that her right hand was pinning the yellow envelope in place under her jacket. "Uh, fine. Just fine. The knee's what's giving me the trouble."

"Knees are very tricky. You'd better be careful."

As Stephie drove away from Melissa's house she felt like kicking herself. If only she'd looked around the room first to see if she could find that envelope of photos! But she had never dreamed they would be sitting out in plain sight. Unfortunately, now when Melissa missed the snapshots, she'd know who had taken them. Stephie hoped she wouldn't miss them anytime soon. It was pretty obvious she wasn't really interested in photography, and Stephie hoped she wouldn't look at the pictures again for a long time. The camera was just another of her toys.

Not that I'm afraid of Melissa, Stephie thought, but there's no telling who she might talk to.

As soon as she got home, Stephie sorted the snapshots into chronological order according to the time stamped on their borders. She laid aside the ones taken between eleven-thirty and midnight. Those were the crucial ones. The newspaper article had placed the time of death at about midnight and she was pretty sure no more than a half hour had elapsed between her fight with Matt and the time of his death.

11:45—a snapshot of Matt in the hallway with Rachel. Matt was leaning against the wall on one hand and was staring down at Rachel. She had one hand raised, palm upward in what might have been a pleading gesture. Caught unaware by the flash, her lips were comically pursed, her eyes too wide. The flash had whitened both their faces, showing that Melissa had been standing close to them when she snapped the picture. That was presumably how she had been able to hear that Matt had rebuffed Rachel.

11:52—Sumir was coming out of the powder room with a shocked look on his face, shocked by nothing more than Melissa's flashbulb popping in his face, probably. Dennis had happened to be passing by then, too. He was so close to the flash his face was bleached white, but she recognized the way he thrust his head forward. She paused at this photo. Sumir had not been sitting on the stairs the entire time as he said. He had taken out time to go to the bathroom. Either he was too shy to mention it or he had forgotten about it. It struck Stephie for the first time that in giving the owner of the truck an alibi, Sumir was giving himself one, too. That was something she'd have to think about.

11:57—J.J., his face also bleached white by the flash, was looking angry with his mouth wide open. She couldn't be sure whether he was shouting at someone, possibly Melissa, or whether he had simply let his mouth fall open when the flash went off. Too bad the pictures didn't come with explanatory captions as well as with the time stamped on them. She could tell that J.J. was in the living room—she recognized the fireplace. Her heart squeezed painfully as she spotted Matt next to the leather chair. He was leaning toward the camera, slightly off balance, his lips parted in a smile that was almost a sneer. His shirt, open almost to the waist, showed his throat in a clean curve of white as if he were deliberately baring his neck to death, completely vulnerable. She winced at the thought. His dark curls were wild and tousled, his eyes were shiny and she had no doubt that he was close to passing out. She supposed the figure standing next to him, back to the camera, must be Jordan. It was, in any event, someone tall with smooth, dark hair, and Jordan was the only guy at the party she could think of who fit that description.

11:59—the shot of Dennis mugging for the camera. Peering at it closely, Stephie could make out that the door behind him, the front door of the house, was ajar. Odd that the door had been left slightly open. In the background Mike Barton, who was Jordan's chief rival on the tennis team, was lifting a beer can to his unnaturally pink lips.

She scanned the photos again, feeling slightly let down. She had the nagging feeling that something was wrong, that she was missing something, but she couldn't figure out what. There were many other snapshots in the pile, but they didn't seem relevant to Matt's death. And the ones taken during the half hour before his death raised more questions than they answered. The one thing she could tell from them was that Matt had been in the living room at 11:57 when the picture of J.J. was taken. Minutes later, he was dead.

He had talked to both Rachel and Jordan just before he died. Unfortunately, he could have talked to any number of other people as well.

Stephie reached for the phone and dialed Mike

Barton's number. It took him a minute to remember who she was since she scarcely knew him, but she explained she was trying to reconstruct the events of the night Matt had died and asked him what he could remember.

"Nothing," he said at once. "The cops asked me all that stuff. I wasn't drunk, either. I nursed one beer all night. I'm just your basic lousy witness."

"You remember Melissa taking pictures, though, don't you?"

"Well, yeah. We all were seeing blue dots because she wouldn't let up."

"Do you remember Dennis cutting up for the camera?"

"Yeah, kind of a clown, isn't he?"

"Try to remember, Mike. Who was in the living room when Dennis was clowning around?"

"Dunno. J.J., of course. No, maybe that was earlier. I can't be sure."

"What about Matt?"

"Yeah, he was there, drunk as a skunk."

"He was watching Dennis clown around?"

"Wait a minute—yeah. No. I'm not sure. Maybe that was before."

"He was sitting in a leather chair in the living room just a few minutes earlier. Was he gone, do you think, by the time Dennis started clowning around?"

"Gee, I don't know. What difference does it make?"

Stephie hung up, swearing under her breath. If all her witnesses were as hopeless as Mike, she was going to get nowhere. She wondered what Dennis would think of the photos. She'd love to go over them with him. It would help get her thoughts organized. She took the photos into the spare room where the computer was. Stephie's father had used the computer in his work, and it was still hooked up to the main computer at his company's Raleigh office. It was one of the few parts of himself he had left at the house after he decided to marry Kimberly, a flight attendant. It was an expensive piece of equipment and she had been surprised he left it, but he had said it would help her with her schoolwork. She guessed he left it to ease the guilt he felt at not being there to help her himself. Sometimes she felt an odd comfort in using it, just like the comfort she got from wrapping herself in her father's old bathrobe when she was alone in the house at night. She liked the computer's inflexible logic, too, and its never varying behavior. Parents might quit loving each other, friends might become murder suspects, but the computer would faithfully present an A prompt every time she booted it up.

She made a careful list of all the relevant photos. Then she made a list of the suspects, and finally clues, such as the last people who had talked to Matt. She made notes of holes in supposed alibis, such as Sumir's visit to the bathroom. And possible motives, too. The last, in particular, made quite a respectable list. Looking at the facts so neatly listed on the screen, she felt she was at last making progress. The problem was she really ought to be working on her American history paper. She could just see herself telling Mrs. Warner that she needed extra time because she'd been busy trying to catch a murderer.

When the phone rang, she jumped guiltily before grabbing it.

"Stephie?" It was Dennis, sounding more than usually embarrassed. "I'm sick of my American history paper, and I've been thinking I'm ready to take a break. Want to go get some pizza?"

"I'd love to," she said and meant it. This would be her chance to show Dennis the photos.

"You would? Great! I mean, that's terrific. I'll be right over. In a few minutes, I mean. Be right there."

Stephie pressed the key to save her notes, then printed two copies, one for her and one for Dennis. She folded them and tucked them in her pocketbook and walked away leaving the computer glowing its reliable A >. She liked listening to its faint hum. It was company in the empty house.

A few minutes later Dennis arrived and began nervously talking about his American history paper. He was acting as uptight as if they were on a date, Stephie realized, which made her feel bad since she only wanted to go over her ideas about the murder with Dennis. He finally sensed her mind wasn't on the American history paper and his stream of chatter faltered. There was a moment of uncomfortable silence before he said, "Have you noticed, it's always something?"

"You mean, like the American history paper?"

"No, I mean like when I was thirteen I kept thinking that when I got rid of my braces and zits my life would be perfect. No such luck."

Stephie laughed. It hit her right then that it was impossible to imagine Matt admitting to braces or zits. Or Jordan, either, for that matter. Dennis seemed so real by comparison. He was so normal. She supposed his parents had made him go to Sunday school and learn to play a musical instrument. No doubt he'd been a Cub Scout. What's more, he would have admitted it without getting embarrassed.

He heaved a sigh and continued, "And now it's this

thing with Matt. I keep thinking we could be having a really good time if it weren't for—"

"Since you bring it up—" Stephie began.

"Of course, that's probably an illusion. I mean, if it wasn't this it would be something else."

"I have something I want to show you."

"Is it about Matt?"

"Sure." She seemed surprised. "I thought that was what we were talking about."

"Figures," he said gloomily.

Once they got inside Pizza Hut, she whipped out the photos. "Just take a look at these."

Dennis's eyes lit at once on the shot of himself mugging for the camera. "Ouch." He winced.

"I think it's cute," said Stephie.

"You do?" His blue eyes were full of hope.

"Uh-huh." She didn't want to lead Dennis on in some unkind way because she liked him—she really did. But all she could think of right then was bringing Matt's killer to justice. "What I'm really interested in," she explained, "is what was going on the last few minutes before midnight."

"Is that when Matt died?"

"According to the newspaper. I don't know how exact that is."

"Well, it should be pretty easy to pin down the time of death." Dennis frowned. "He obviously hadn't been dead long when we called nine-one-one. That was at midnight and I remember noticing that Brad had fresh blood on his fingers."

Stephie gripped the edge of the table as black-and-white pinwheels spun before her eyes.

"Are you okay?" Dennis asked anxiously.

She nodded but didn't trust herself to speak.

"If it gets to you so much, Stephie, why do you keep at it?"

"I've got to know what happened, that's why. I guess you think I'm weird."

"No-o." He was considering her thoughtfully.

"Well, I don't care if you do."

"You haven't told anybody else what you're up to, have you?"

"Of course not." Uneasily she remembered the newspapers she had left spread all over the library table and the fact that Melissa knew why she wanted the snapshots. But she couldn't worry about every little thing or she'd freeze and wouldn't be able to act. She picked up the snapshot of Dennis. "Can you remember who was in the room with you when Melissa took this?"

He shrugged. "Melissa, of course."

Stephie blinked. She had forgotten all about Melissa. Whenever a picture had been taken, Melissa had been there taking it. The pictures provided a more complete account of Melissa's whereabouts than anybody's.

Dennis looked again at the picture and whistled. "I see, the time is stamped on here. This must have been just before it happened."

"I think it was. Was Matt in the living room then?"

"I don't know, Stephie. The police asked me all that stuff, too, but I couldn't remember for the life of me. I kept seeing him different places all night, generally making an ass of himself . . ." Dennis blushed. Stephie wondered if he was telling the truth. He wouldn't have been human if he hadn't kept an eye on Matt. It must have crossed his mind that the way Matt was behaving maybe increased his chances of getting somewhere with Matt's girlfriend.

"You truly don't remember?" she insisted.

"I really don't. I'd hate to swear to anything."

"Nobody seems to remember where anybody was." Stephie ran her fingers through her hair despairingly. "And we're talking about such a short time. It wouldn't take long for Matt to step outside." She frowned. "What really bothers me is I can't figure out why he went out."

"Must have been a girl."

"Why do you say that?"

"No reason to go outside with a guy, right? Might have wanted to go someplace private with a girl, though."

Stephie gathered up the photos. She didn't like the idea, but she had to consider it. Was it possible that Matt had left the party with Rachel? They had just had a big fight, according to Melissa. Could Rachel have somehow lured him outside? It seemed unlikely.

"Of course, somebody could have invited him to step outside and fight," Dennis added. "Hadn't thought about that."

"Matt never got in fistfights."

"Probably afraid he'd spoil his pretty face." Stephie's expression made him flush again. "I'm sorry. Heck, I know the guy is dead, Stephie, but I don't have to pretend I liked him just because of that."

"No-o." She stacked the photographs. "I know he wasn't always nice. But one-on-one he was a different person."

"I really don't want to hear about it."

Stephie understood. She had hated to hear Matt talk about Rachel. She abruptly changed the subject. "What I keep coming back to is that it wasn't like Matt to leave a party early."

"Yeah, but I hear he'd been fighting with practically

everyone all night. You could hardly find anybody he didn't insult. Maybe the party got too hot for him."

"Maybe." She sighed. "I keep having the feeling that something is wrong with these pictures but I've looked at them a hundred times and can't figure out what. It's like seeing something out of the corner of my eye, but when I turn to focus on it, it's not there."

"Maybe your subconscious is working on it, and it'll come to you in a sudden burst of insight."

"I hope so, but I'm not counting on it. I'm not exactly overflowing with insights lately. I think we ought to try going at this from the point of view of motive."

"But what if it really was an accident, Stephie? Accidents don't have motives."

"I don't agree it was an accident, okay? For one thing, Matt was practically the only person at that party who was really drunk."

"You think?"

"Yes. It suddenly came to me that the only person who was stumbling drunk enough to drive over Matt by accident was Matt himself." She smiled bleakly. "And I think we can let him out."

"You may be right. I expect one beer slows your reflexes and all, but to drive over somebody and then run your truck into a ditch, that's more than a little drunk."

She handed him a copy of her computer printout. "You can keep this one," she said. "I'll just run off another." He scanned it quickly.

"Sumir?" he yelped. "What possible motive could Sumir have?"

"He wasn't exactly sorry to replace Matt on the Quiz Bowl team, was he? You heard him say how important it was to have things to put down on a college application."

"Yeah, but come on!"

"I have to put everything down if I'm going to have a complete list. Next there was Rachel. When she tried to make up with Matt—according to Melissa—he was nasty to her. Melissa also said he argued with Jordan that night. Jordan was one of the last people to see him after he told Jordan he was backing out of their trip to Europe, just so Jordan wouldn't get to go. His parents won't let him go alone."

"Seems like a lot of this depends on Melissa's say-so."

"I've got Melissa on the list, too," Stephie pointed out. "Matt always used to say she cheated on the Quiz Bowl exam so she could get on the team to be near Jordan. For all we know Matt threatened to expose her."

Dennis put his napkin on his head and grinned. "Hey, I don't know how to tell you this, but I don't think it's something Melissa would kill for."

"Oh, I know that. I don't seriously suspect Melissa. But somebody did it, Dennis. Matt's dead."

"Let's be reasonable, okay? For argument's sake, I'll agree that Matt was murdered. What kind of motive can anybody really have to murder a sixteen-year-old kid?"

"What if J.J. has a violent side nobody knows about? What if he's a split personality?"

The napkin on Dennis's head slid to the floor. He looked amused. "You're putting me on."

"Check item five on the motive list," suggested Stephie.

"Where'd you come up with an idea like that?"

"Well, you have to admit he *was* acting pretty weird at regionals. He practically came right out and told me he was falling apart."

Dennis whistled soundlessly. "Seriously?"

"He said sometimes he didn't know who he was."

"I don't know, Stephie. It seems pretty farfetched to me."

Stephie frowned. "What really bothers me is there are probably lots of other motives we don't know about. Matt was always interested in other people's secrets. You know, how he seemed to know everything that was going on. It was like he had special antennae for picking up on what other people were up to."

"Nosy."

"Well, curious, anyway. I keep thinking he could have stumbled on something he shouldn't have known about."

Dennis grinned. "The mob, huh?"

Stephie sighed. "Oh, I know. It's just an idea. I mean, if he was blackmailing somebody, he'd have to have evidence. Gossip wouldn't be enough. He would have needed something solid—something in writing. Or witnesses. I wonder how we could find out." Stephie bit her lip. Maybe evidence like that could be hidden in Matt's room still—if it ever existed. Presumably a real detective would make up some excuse to go into Matt's bedroom and search, but it was no use pretending she could look Mrs. Howell in the face and tell her a flat lie. There was no point in even thinking about it.

"I don't know, Stephie," Dennis admitted. "It all sounds like a made-for-TV movie. Do you honestly think Matt could have been a blackmailer?"

There was a long silence. Stephie could hear the

jukebox playing and little children giggling at the next table. "I don't know," she admitted.

"He sounds like a real prince of a fellow. His own girlfriend thinks he blackmailed his friends."

She doodled concentric circles on the back of the envelope. "I don't think that. Not really. But he was insecure and that made him do strange things sometimes. And, well, he did have kind of a thing about wanting power."

The waitress slid their pizza onto the metal serving dish. After she left Dennis said, "I'll lay you odds this turns out to be an accident after all. It just doesn't make sense that somebody murdered him. Things like that don't happen."

"You may be right." Stephie bit into her pizza and let a trail of mozzarella stretch almost to the point of breaking.

"But you don't believe me."

"Nope." The strand of mozzarella snapped.

There was a long silence, which Dennis finally broke. "I don't like it, and I'll tell you what I don't like about it. If somebody we know did kill him, then that person must be totally insane."

"Maybe—maybe not. We have come up with a couple of perfectly sane reasons why somebody might have wanted Matt out of the way."

"Well, keep in mind that if you're right about all this, and the murderer really did push you off that landing, you're in serious trouble."

"I'm going to be very careful."

"I hope so." But he eyed her doubtfully.

It's a long shot, thought the murderer, sitting alone in front of the computer. But long shots have always been lucky for me. The murderer flipped open a black address book, checked a penciled number next to Stephie's name, dialed it and put the phone in the modem and watched the lit-up computer screen.

RING

RING

RING

CONNECT

I'm in, thought the murderer gleefully. No junk about passwords with Stephie's computer. The idea probably hadn't even occurred to her. A directory of files. Piece of cake. It wasn't long before a single word stood out on the computer screen as if highlighted.

MURDER

A faint smile played on the murderer's face. Stephie was exactly the type who would title a file Murder. She was straightforward to the point of stupidity. Nothing subtle about her. The smile disappeared. Unfortunately, this file showed she was serious. Stealing those photographs, reading those old newspaper stories, even calling up Mike Barton—she seemed to think she was a hotshot detective. She must be living out some Nancy Drew fantasy.

When the file titled Murder was called up on the screen, it turned out to be a list of suspects. The whole Quiz Bowl team had made the list, so it wasn't as if she had narrowed it down. But the timetable and the list of motives that followed made the murderer's blood run cold. She was getting close. Too close. What a nerve! The murderer's breathing became shallow and quick. Ruin my life, will she? Smash my future to bits just because of one little moment that I overstepped the line. No way. I won't let it happen.

That settles it. The girl has got to go. No more halfway attempts. This time she has to be taken out—and soon. Before she can do any damage.

11

When Dennis dropped Stephie off at her house, it was dark, and the streetlights had come on.

"Is that a cop car?" asked Dennis.

Stephie did a double take. Sure enough, the police were parked in front of her neighbor's house. "I wonder what's going on. They're parked in front of the Whites' house."

"Want me to hang around till you find out?"

"Don't bother. It's probably nothing."

"See you, then." He touched her arm gently. "Be careful."

"Careful is my middle name." Despite Stephie's confident words, she had to admit that a police car in the neighborhood wasn't exactly reassuring. As soon as she got inside, she called the Whites to find out what was going on.

Mrs. White was only too glad to tell her. "Somebody broke in! Jerome is out of town and I had to work late. I only got in a quarter of an hour ago, but I knew something was wrong the minute I walked in—even before I turned on the lights. I could feel a cold wind whistling through the house! I knew a window was out. So I went right back to my bedroom and called the police."

Stephie was sure that if she opened the front door and realized her house had been broken into, the last thing she would have done would be to go in. What if the burglar had still been there?

"They threw a cement block through the kitchen window and crawled in over the broken glass," said Mrs. White. "I'm as sure as I can be that it was one of those dope fiends. No normal person crawls over broken glass. I just don't know how I'm going to get to sleep tonight. You be careful. Jerome and I really worry about you being over there alone all week. You know, this is the fourth house he's broken into."

"The fourth house?" Stephie repeated numbly. She had had no idea. She had been so caught up in her murder investigation that she hadn't noticed the crime wave in progress in her own neighborhood. She vaguely remembered that Melissa had mentioned a series of break-ins in her neighborhood. The burglars must be working their way across the town. "They hit the Watsons on Black Pearl Cove and the Azernoks next door to them," said Mrs. White. "And last week it was the Ortegas on Lagoon Terrace. Every time the burglary was in broad daylight. I guess they know that this is a neighborhood where almost everyone works. Daytime would be the safest time to break in around here."

If the burglars were breaking in during the day, Stephie reasoned, she would be perfectly safe. But even so—she suddenly felt there was something spooky about being alone in her house. Her mom wouldn't be home until the weekend.

"We're getting a burglar alarm," Mrs. White announced.

"That sounds like a wonderful idea," said Stephie.

After she hung up, she took a deep breath and reminded herself that she was going to have to handle this on her own as best she could. She flipped open the yellow pages and checked the heading under burglar alarms. It was too late to call, but she'd get on it first thing tomorrow morning.

A few moments later Stephie's mom called, and Stephie filled her in on the neighborhood burglaries. "Go ahead and look into the burglar alarms," Mrs. Yates agreed. "But don't panic. Did you notice that all the people they've hit so far have houses on the golf course?"

Stephie hadn't thought of it, but she realized her mother was right. The Azernoks, for example, were continually complaining about golf balls in their backyard. And the Whites, across the street, were practically on the driving range.

"That's probably because with those houses they can come up behind the house by way of the golf course and carry stuff off without being seen," suggested her mother.

The idea of burglars tooling along the golf course in a golf cart stuffed with televisions and stereos seemed irresistibly funny to Stephie and she began to giggle.

"The police will be patroling, too," her mother reminded her. "They'll be on the lookout from now on."

Stephie felt reassured. Their house wasn't a likely target. Not only was it not on the golf course, but it also had a small lake directly behind it, which blocked access from the back. Reasoning this out, Stephie began to feel better.

The next morning when she left for school, she spotted a police cruiser driving slowly down the street. Really, she decided, there was nothing to worry about. She was as safe as could be. Or as safe as anyone pursuing a murder investigation could be, she reminded herself.

When Stephie got to school, she pulled into her usual parking place and Rachel greeted her merrily. "Hey, I read in the paper about all those burglaries in your neighborhood. Doesn't it make you nervous being all alone?"

Two parking spaces away from Stephie, Jordan unfolded his long legs awkwardly from his Corvette. "Cut it out, Rachel. You want to make the girl a nervous wreck?"

"I'm not telling her anything she doesn't know!" said Rachel. "The paper said four burglaries in two weeks. They just throw a concrete block through a big window and walk right in."

Melissa struggled out of the Corvette's passenger seat carrying her heavy book bag. "It's terrible," she said. "My dad says when he was growing up around here, people never even locked their doors. Now practically every house in our neighborhood has a burglar alarm."

"I'm thinking of having a burglar alarm put in," Stephie said.

"That's the worst thing you can do," Rachel assured her. "I knew these people who lived out by the reservoir who had every sort of state-of-the-art burglar alarm and they got broken into three times. My theory is that burglar alarms just make crooks think you've got something worth stealing."

What did Rachel expect her to do? wondered Stephie. Pull the covers over her head and cry? She felt she had to take some sort of action. "I called three different companies and they're all sending somebody out to give me an estimate this afternoon."

"Well, go ahead and have one put in," said Rachel, "if it will make you feel better." Her tone implied that all efforts were futile.

Later that afternoon after Stephie talked to the burglar alarm experts, she was ready to agree with Rachel. Three different firms sent their representatives to the house. Each expert was tall, relaxed, and dressed in tan chinos. They might have been clones. The systems they were selling were ingenious. One company sold pads to hide under the carpet, which were set off by a burglar's stepping on them. Another system picked up vibrations and went off if anyone tried to jimmy a door or window. Yet another shone invisible beams over every door or window in the house and went off if the beam was broken by the thief's entry. There were even systems that picked up any movement in the yard and automatically turned on floodlights and sirens so that quiet suburban lawns would look like prison yards during escape attempts.

Stephie's mother called that night to check on her progress. "I don't know," Stephie said doubtfully. "Every burglar alarm man I have out here tells me what's wrong with the other guy's systems, and they all cost a fortune. The cheapest one is over a thousand dollars. But that's not the worst part."

"Then what's the worst part, pray tell?"

"They all finish up by saying the same thing," Stephie reported grimly. " 'If he really wants to get in, he's going to get in.' "

"Oh, dear."

Just then, a jangling sound began ringing with nerve-wracking regularity. "What's that?" her mother cried.

"It's the Whites' burglar alarm."

"Do you want to hang up and call the police or something?"

"No," said Stephie. "It's been going off all afternoon. They just had it put in this morning. That's something I didn't mention. Thunder sets off the alarms, lightning sets them off, dogs set them off, and as far as I can tell half the time they just go off for no reason. Mrs. White says lots of the neighbors are getting them now."

"I see." Her mother hesitated. "Well, I think we need to keep calm, Stephie. Even if someone does break into the house, God forbid, the insurance will cover it. And the break-ins are happening only during the day when you're gone."

Stephie agreed. She knew her mother was thinking that they couldn't afford to lay out thousands for a burglar alarm.

Late that night when Stephie was in bed, the Whites' burglar alarm went off once again. It was so loud she had to cover her ears and it seemed to clamor forever into the lonely emptiness of the neighborhood. No neighbors opened their doors to see what was up. No police drove up with blinking blue lights. It was as if the alarm were proof of the indifference of the world. It was silenced a few minutes later, but by then Stephie was completely unnerved.

Suddenly the phone rang. Startled, Stephie grabbed for it. The luminous dial on her clock said eleven. Could her mother have been in an accident?

"Hello?" she asked anxiously. She heard a click at the other end. "Hello?" She hung up, her heart squeezing with fear. Probably a wrong number, she told herself. But she couldn't rid herself of the menace that seemed to hang over her darkened room. Stephie remembered Matt's body lying under the ominous white sheet and found she could scarcely move she had become so frightened. Perhaps some unknown man was at that very moment lurking in the bushes outside. Matt's murderer, the caller, and the burglar blurred in her mind to form a single malign force. Someone was stalking her. He had only called to be sure she was at home. She sat up suddenly, her teeth chattering as she turned on the light. Then she slid out of bed and padded barefoot into the kitchen. At least the blinds were closed so she didn't have to worry that someone was watching her. Nervously she checked both the front and back doors to make sure they were locked. The words of the burglar alarm men kept echoing in her head. "If he wants to get in, he's going to get in."

She wished there wasn't so much glass in the house. Because of the fine view out over the lake in the back, the house had been built with a sliding glass door in her mother's room and huge floor-to-ceiling windows in the dining area. Stephie remembered that the burglar had gotten in the Whites' house by throwing a cement block through the window. It seemed almost futile to bother locking the doors when she was living in what amounted to a glass house.

She poured milk into a mug and put it in the microwave. Then she sat at the kitchen table listening to the comforting hum of the oven. She was bound to hear any breaking glass, and if someone broke in she could call the police. Unless he cut the phone lines! She picked up the kitchen phone in a panic and was relieved to hear a dial tone. She was perfectly safe as long as she was awake, but she couldn't stay awake all night.

At three A.M. she fell into bed, too tired to keep her eyes open.

12

"Y ou look terrible," Rachel said to Stephie the next morning in the parking lot. "Maybe you're coming down with something."

"No. It's just that I'm not sleeping," Stephie said wearily. "All those burglaries. To top it off, I got one of those wrong numbers where the person just hangs up."

"That's awful!" cried Rachel. "I couldn't stand being alone like that at night! You must be scared out of your mind."

Stephie noticed that her hand was not too steady and quickly bent down and pretended to rearrange the books in her book bag until Rachel left. She didn't want to walk to class with Rachel talking about the burglaries.

Dennis hailed her and galloped over to her car. "Hey, Stephie, I've been thinking."

"Let's get in the car to talk," she said. "It's cold out here."

With some difficulty, Stephie got back in the driver's seat—her knee was still hurting. Dennis slid in beside her. "I've been thinking maybe we're going about this all wrong," he said. "What we need to do is work up a psychological profile of the killer."

"Does this mean you're starting to believe me?"

"I guess so. Sorta." He looked uncomfortable. "Anyway, this is what occurred to me. The murderer couldn't have known that Matt was going to get drunk, right?"

"I guess you're right."

"So the murderer couldn't count on it. Unless he, or she, was giving Matt the liquor."

Stephie shook her head. "Forget that. I was with him all night."

"So you might say the murderer just took advantage of the situation. He couldn't have planned it ahead of time. It would have been the same way with you getting pushed off that landing. He couldn't have counted on the lights going out."

"They did flicker a time or two, first," Stephie reminded him.

"Yeah, but suppose they'd gone out when you were in the cafeteria? Or safe in your room? Pushing you had to be done on an impulse. Do you see what I'm getting at? Like it couldn't have been Sumir because he plans everything. If he'd done it there'd be a list somewhere that said 'do history homework, format new disks, push Stephie off landing."

"You're saying the murderer is somebody who thinks on his feet."

"Right!"

"Not like Melissa, in other words."

"Oh, I don't know. I've never thought Melissa was as dumb as she acts. It's just her image—dumb Melissa. She probably thinks boys like it or something. I notice lots of times people end up helping her do things because they think she can't cope. As images go, dumbness is not such a bad deal."

"You can't honestly suspect Melissa, Dennis! It's ridiculous. She's the one who warned me that the railing was low."

"That shows she'd noticed, huh?"

"Also she practically freaked out about the lights going out. She was afraid. Really rattled."

"You'd almost think something was preying on her mind, wouldn't you?" purred Dennis.

"I just can't see Melissa as a murderer," Stephie said firmly. "I figure that the murderer is someone for whom action is second nature."

"J.J.?"

"Well, you have to admit he's the one who's been acting weird."

"That doesn't mean he did it. The fact is, Stephie, we don't know who did it. All we know is he's like a rattlesnake. He strikes first and thinks later."

"So far he's been careful to make his attempts look like accidents."

"So you should watch for anything unusual— anything the murderer could use. Matt being drunk, the lights going out—those were both unexpected bonuses that the killer turned to his advantage."

"Don't worry. I'm going to stay away from balconies, open windows, speeding cars, champagne bottles—"

"Champagne bottles?"

"Haven't you ever read the warnings about aiming the cork well away from you?"

"Sorry, my drink is apple juice."

"My parents always had champagne on their anniversary," said Stephie wistfully.

Dennis bent toward her. "Hey, don't be sad."

Stephie could see that he was about to kiss her and she panicked. She glanced at her watch, saw it was time for the bell, and suddenly flung her car door open. "We're going to be late!"

Stephie couldn't even run for it because of her bad knee, so she urged Dennis to go on without her. She was glad when, after a moment's hesitation, he did. She limped painfully toward the main building. Sherlock Holmes certainly didn't have problems like this. If only Dennis would concentrate on the murder instead of on her! That intense look in his blue eyes made her want to bolt. She wasn't ready to get involved.

She was three minutes late to homeroom, but she had used those three minutes well. Dennis had given her something to think about. He had intentionally or unintentionally suggested a psychological profile of the killer. She had been wasting time looking for solid clues, but Dennis had made her realize there was another way to look at it. What sort of person would commit this kind of murder?

The murderer had a very characteristic way of acting. Now that she was focusing on that, Stephie felt she was much closer to figuring out who the murderer was.

13

When Stephie's mother called that night, Stephie announced she was thinking of buying a large dog. "I'm all for it," said Mrs. Yates. "I just hate it that I can't be at home with you."

"I'm fine, Mom, really. What could you do if you were here?"

"We'd both feel better, that's all."

Stephie knew it was true, but she didn't want to admit it out loud. These days, since her parents had split, Stephie's first instinct was to protect her mother. That was why it was only after some hesitation that she mentioned the anonymous phone call.

"And he didn't say anything?"

"Just a click."

"Probably a wrong number. I've gotten that kind of call. I guess the person's embarrassed he woke you up."

Stephie admitted that she, too, had picked up such calls before, but somehow this one was different.

"You sound worried, Stephie. Are you sure you're okay? Should I come home?"

"No. No, I'm fine, Mom."

"If it happens again, have the police put a tracer on the phone."

"That's a good idea," said Stephie, relieved that there was some action she could take.

"Okay, honey, I'll be home soon. I love you."

"I love you, too." Stephie felt all choked up when she placed the receiver back in its place. This was all her father's fault, she thought. On an impulse, she picked up the phone again and dialed his number.

"Kimberly and I cannot come to the phone right now, but if you will leave a brief message at the sound of the tone, we will return your call as soon as possible," said the answering machine.

Stephie slammed the receiver down. She knew that likely as not her father was working late and Kimberly the airhead was working out at a gym, trying to stay under the airline's weight requirement. But she couldn't escape the feeling that her father had gone off to have a good time, leaving her and her mom in the soup. She could call back and leave a message on his answering machine, she supposed. "Hi, Dad, this is Stephie. I've been pushed off a second-floor landing, have had a burglar in my bedroom, and now I'm being stalked by a murderer, but don't let it ruin your day." But she didn't want any of that stuff about the murder to get back to her mother. Likely as not her mother would get so worried she couldn't work and then what would they do for money? Besides, a frantic message to her father would only lead to messy scenes. Her dad would start insisting that she come to live with him and Kimberly—and that was the last thing she wanted. Stephie opened the refrigerator and stared at the contents. She wasn't really hungry. She decided to do her homework, try to catch the last bit of "Jeopardy," and get some sleep. She'd feel better the next day.

She toyed with the idea of sleeping in her jeans, but in the end, she put on her pajamas. At first the simple actions of her normal routine reassured her. She climbed into bed at eleven and lay there studying the patterns the streetlight made as it leaked through the venetian blinds.

The phone rang. She stared at it, fascinated, wondering if she should pick it up. Suddenly, unable to stand the suspense any longer, she grabbed it. "Hello?" she gasped. The caller clicked the receiver down. With a trembling hand, Stephie replaced hers. Someone was out there. Someone knew she was alone. She pulled the covers up to her chin. She listened hard, holding her breath, waiting for any sound that would mean someone was trying to get into the house. Then she got up and crept around the house, checking every door. The microwave clock glowed 11:20 in the dark kitchen. The hum of the refrigerator stopped suddenly. It was so quiet that her mind began to invent sounds. The stillness of the house was unnerving. She was cold in her thin pajamas and soon crawled back into bed, where she sat for a long time hugging her knees and shivering. At last, dizzy with fatigue, she switched off the light. She couldn't go on like this, she thought. She had to sleep.

She turned her pillow over and over, trying to arrange it into a comfortable shape, but it was no use. She felt lumps no matter which way she lay. Much later when she was staring at the patterns of light on the ceiling, a thought struck her that chilled her.

Dennis had said watch out for anything unusual. These neighborhood burglaries were unusual. What if the murderer, under cover of the burglaries broke into her house? If she were killed now, everyone would say it had been done by the burglars. She lay stiffly on her back, her mouth so dry that her tongue stuck to the roof of her mouth. Matt's killer must know she was looking for him. Now he would be stalking her. She lay there a long time, turning everything she knew about Matt's murder over in her head.

Suddenly she heard the sharp crash of breaking glass, then a collapsing tinkle as glass fell, a sound frightening in its finality. Her breath sucked in and she couldn't breathe. She fumbled for the phone but the receiver fell from her grasp and clunked against the bedside table. Afraid the entire phone would fall next, she grabbed it with both her hands. Still scarcely breathing, she listened, expecting to hear sounds from her mother's room. But there were no sounds of drawers and closets being opened. Instead a hinge creaked. In her mother's bedroom, directly next to hers, the door was being opened very slowly.

Quickly, Stephie slid from under the covers, groping for the floor with her bare feet. As she lifted her weight off the bed, it creaked with a sound like a shriek. Her heart beat wildly in her throat as she lay down on the carpet and scooted under her bed, pushing aside a cardboard box of summer clothes with an impatient thrust of her leg. The dust ruffle fluttered then fell back into place. She lay there, perfectly still, her nose tickling from dust.

Then she heard the soft metallic click of the knob of her bedroom door being turned. This was no ordinary burglar, her brain screamed. He was stalking her! She was trapped. She couldn't believe she had been so stupid as to get under the bed. She could have wept with frustration. She saw too late that she should have taken a chair and crashed it through her front bedroom window. She could have jumped out of the house screaming. Anything would have been better than to lie there on her back with cold sweat running between her shoulder blades. She could hear his steps as he came in, the faint brushing whisper of sneakers on carpet. It was only a few steps from the door to her bed. Then he stopped, evidently stymied by the sight of the comforter thrown back on the empty bed. Stephie clenched her teeth, willing herself to be still. She heard the doors of her closet being slid open, and her heart seemed to stop beating. Perhaps he was only searching for valuables, after all. But the closet slid shut again and then there was no sound. The murderer must be standing still in the middle of her room.

She knew it was the murderer. He was looking for her and in a moment he had to peek under her bed. Desperate, she gently fingered the side of the bed, testing it. If he bent to peer under the bed, could she possibly push the bed over and throw him off balance? But as soon as she touched the solid wood of the old bed, Stephie knew it was hopeless. She had crawled into a trap. She was in a tightly restricted position, flat on her back. The bed would be too heavy for her to move.

The dust ruffle lifted and Stephie's eyes flew open wide in terror. Suddenly a loud jangle rent the air—insistent, monotonous—the Whites' burglar alarm. It filled her skull with a terrifying noise, so loud in the quiet night that it might have been right in her room.

"Damn!" Something about the voice was elusively familiar, Stephie thought, startled. The intruder hesitated a moment, then the door to the bedroom was pulled open with such force that the dust ruffle fluttered. In his headlong flight the intruder did not close the door behind him and Stephie heard him charging through her mother's room. A clunk and then a grunt. He had hit something. He was no longer bothering to be quiet. He had panicked. She heard his foot crunch on the broken glass and then nothing. A few minutes later more shards of glass fell into the silence.

She lay there, too frightened to move. The Whites' alarm had stopped, and she became conscious that her room was colder. The dust ruffle fluttered a bit. The shattered glass in her mother's room must be letting cold air blow through the house. She inched out from under the bed, breathing heavily, and crept to the door of her bedroom and turned to peer into her mother's room. She could see only the faint outlines of the furniture. She couldn't bring herself to turn on the light. She got her coat out of the hall closet and put it on over her pajamas. Then she slipped on her shoes. She cracked the front door slightly and peeked out, ready to slam it shut if she saw anyone suspicious out front, but the streetlight in front of her house shone only on the white gravel of the driveway and the familiar cars of the neighborhood. The mulberry tree under the light, its branches moved by the night breezes, cast a moving shadow.

Stephie was relieved to see that a square of yellow light across the street showed that the Whites were in their kitchen. They must have gotten up to turn off the alarm. Holding her coat together with both hands, she ran down the front steps and across the street and banged on their door. "Mrs. White! Mrs. White!" she screamed.

Mr. White threw open the front door, staring at her aghast. "Stephie! What's wrong?"

"The burglar!" she gasped. "He just broke into my house."

"My word! The burglar's over at Stephie's house, Doris."

"I think he's gone now." Stephie stepped inside the house, shivering now from head to foot. The Whites' cat arched his back and eyed her with suspicion.

Mrs. White appeared, her gray hair sticking up in odd places. She was wearing a green bathrobe wrapped around a long flannel nightgown. Her face was lined and drawn. "Are you all right, dear?" She hugged Stephie. "Don't just stand there like a dummy, Jerome. Call the police."

Stephie let herself be led into the kitchen where she collapsed in a chair and let the Whites' solicitude wash over her. Her knee was throbbing. She made no move to take off her coat. She felt she would never be warm again.

The familiarity of the intruder's voice haunted her. She knew it, she was sure, but it nagged at her mind, just out of reach.

The Whites would not hear of her returning to her house that night. They made up a bed for Stephie on their couch. To her surprise, when the police arrived they promised to have the glass in the sliding glass door repaired at once. They said that regulations insisted the house be made "secure" before they left. Stephie doubted that she would ever again feel a sliding glass door was secure.

After the police left, she scarcely slept, tossing and turning on the Whites' couch. Certainly, she didn't dream. Finally, through a dim haze of fatigue, she heard water running and realized that must mean the Whites were up and getting dressed for work. She rapped gently on their bedroom door.

Mrs. White's head peeked out.

"I'm going home, now," Stephie said.

"Are you sure you're all right?" asked Mrs. White anxiously.

"I'm fine. I'd better get ready for school."

"Don't you want breakfast first?"

Stephie shook her head.

The cat sat on the piano and watched as she tugged the sheets off the couch and folded them up neatly.

Then she padded across the street, chilled even though her coat was wrapped around her thin pajamas. She reflected that she seemed to spend a lot of time reassuring people that she was all right. Actually, she felt shivery and uncertain, as if she might burst into tears any minute.

When she peeked into her mother's room, she saw that the glass people had already come and gone. She had to admit to feeling comforted that the glass had been swept up and the plate-glass panel of the door replaced. To look at it now, no one would guess it had been burglarized. The easy chair in front of the television had been knocked askew by the intruder in his flight. Except for that, it appeared as if nothing had been touched. The police had urged her to check to see what was missing, but Stephie knew the intruder had not ransacked the house. She had listened to his every move.

This burglar didn't come for televisions. He had come to kill her. She couldn't say that to the police, though. She knew she couldn't present her theory to the police until she had some evidence. She was back to needing a solid clue. Too bad the burglar hadn't been so obliging as to drop a monogrammed handkerchief.

Stephie fixed herself an English muffin and a glass of milk. When she went back to get dressed, she stood at the door of her room a moment, puzzled. Something was missing. She just couldn't figure out what. Then she stood at the foot of her bed and checked the room from a different angle. The bright splash of yellow she had unconsciously become accustomed to seeing was missing, she realized. The packet of photographs she had taken from Melissa's had been lying on her bureau—now, it was gone.

As Stephie drove to school her mind was in turmoil. When she drove into the school parking lot, she was relieved to see that Dennis's old car had pulled in just ahead of hers. She took the parking space right next to his and jumped out of her car, wincing as pain shot through her knee. "Dennis!"

He turned at the sound of her voice and his eyes lit up. "Stephie!" He saw at once that something was wrong. "What's the matter?"

Stephie poured out the story of the burglary in a rush.

"Calm down," he said. "It's over. It's okay. You didn't get hurt, did you?"

"No." Stephie shivered. "But, Dennis, I don't think it was a burglar. It was the murderer."

"You're kidding!"

"When the neighbor's alarm went off, I guess his nerve cracked or something." She swallowed. "He said 'Damn' and then took off. He was practically running. He ran into a chair in Mom's room. I heard him crash into it."

"You mean he said something? Did you recognize his voice?"

"I almost did. It's like something tickling at the back of my mind. I've almost got it but not quite. You know how it is if somebody just says one word. Like on the phone, sometimes even if it's your best friend, if all she says is 'Hi,' you might not realize who it is. If only he had said a few more words, I know I could have recognized who it was."

"Are you *sure?*"

"I'm not sure about anything," said Stephie. "I'm mostly just scared. But the other burglaries were in the daytime. This was after midnight and this time the burglar took only one thing—Melissa's photographs."

Dennis whistled. "You sure you didn't just lose them?"

She shook her head. "They're gone."

"Did you tell the police?"

"What's the use? *You* don't even believe me. What's the chance the police would believe me?"

"Tell you what, Stephie. I'll ask my mom if you can come stay at our house until this guy is rounded up."

"Oh, Dennis, that is sweet, but I can't—"

Rachel got out of her Mazda. "Hey, did you hear, Stephie? They caught that burglar in your neighborhood."

Stephie gaped at her.

"Where'd you hear that?" asked Dennis.

"On the radio just now. It was on the eight o'clock news. They've charged him with about a hundred burglaries. Some were over in Melissa's neighborhood, too. He was living in a warehouse downtown. He's a cocaine addict, they say." Rachel stared at them expectantly. "Well, isn't that great that they've caught him?"

"Great," said Stephie in a hollow voice.

"Now we don't have to worry anymore," said Rachel.

Stephie exchanged a glance with Dennis. "I better go. If I'm late for homeroom again, I'll get detention."

Dennis walked beside her as she limped toward the main building. "I'll call my mom at lunch," he insisted, "and you can go home with me right after school."

Stephie gripped her book bag tightly. "No, it's sweet of you, Dennis, but if they've caught the burglar, I don't have anything to worry about."

"But I thought you said you were sure of"—he glanced around warily—"you know."

"Yes, but don't you see? He can't risk breaking into my house now. He only did it because he knew everyone would think it was just one of the burglaries we've been having. That would cover his tracks. Now that the burglar's been caught, he won't dare."

"I wouldn't want to bet my life on it," muttered Dennis.

"I just wish I could ask Melissa who else she showed that package of photographs to. But I don't see how I can because she'd know right away that I took them and I'm not ready to admit it." She sighed. "She probably showed them to tons of people anyway."

"Look, Stephie, whether Melissa is mad at you is the least of your troubles. What about concentrating on keeping yourself from getting killed, huh?"

"It's going to be all right," she insisted.

Dennis grabbed her arm. "Okay," he said, "but listen, if you change your mind, just give me a call. I'll be over there to get you in ten minutes. Even if you just get lonely—call."

"Okay."

"Promise you will?" Dennis's eyes were unhappy.

"I promise."

On the way to homeroom, Stephie ran smack into J.J. His book bag fell to the floor with a thud and the zipper snapped open, spilling out a textbook and a couple of spiral notebooks. "Damn!" he muttered.

Stephie's flesh rose into goose bumps. Was it because of her unconscious memory of the voice of the intruder? She backed away and at once bumped into a guy with a shaved head. "Hey!" he yelped.

"You're a regular traffic hazard, Stephie." Frowning, J.J. stooped to pick up his books. "What's the matter with you?"

"N-nothing."

He scowled. "Well, try watching where you're going next time. Keep this up and you're going to get hurt."

J.J. stuffed his books back in. The bag gaped open at the top where the zipper had given way. Stephie stared at his arms as he effortlessly tossed the heavy book bag over one shoulder. A couple of long veins bulged, faintly blue, under his skin, and his shirtsleeve was taut over the muscle. Suddenly he grabbed her shoulder and roughly spun her around. "Walk *with* the traffic, for pete's sake, Stephie. Move." He shoved her so hard, she almost lost her balance. Casting a frightened glance behind her, she slithered through the closely pressed bodies that filled the hall. Soon she was well ahead of him and breathing easier.

She had never seen J.J. so angry. Maybe he was mad she was still alive, she thought, raising a hand to her cheek. She wondered how he had planned to kill her. She knew it would be easy for him to break her neck.

When she reached her homeroom, she fell into her desk, her bad knee throbbing. She had to trust her instincts on this one, she realized. Her conscious mind couldn't make the connection, but her body had responded to the sound of J.J.'s voice with unmistakable fear. She knew who Matt's murderer was now, hard though it was to believe. She didn't know why she was so surprised. She had noticed before how well J.J. fit the psychological profile Dennis had constructed. Nobody was more a creature of action than J.J. She had observed him flexing his muscles or doing chin-ups any place there was a handhold. He was an incredibly physical person, just the sort who would act instinctively. He must think ordinary rules didn't apply to him. She had read about athletes like that— guys who cheated and got in trouble with the law. Athletes got showered with praise and were given special treatment and it ruined them. Not that she had ever noticed any signs of character decay in J.J. before, but now that the veneer was stripped away she saw his violent streak. Maybe he was cracking up. But whatever the reason, she knew he had changed.

The problem was she had no proof, no solid evidence—she kept coming back to that. It did her no good to know who the murderer was unless she could persuade the police he was guilty. And she knew it wouldn't be easy. It was hard even for her to believe that J.J. had murdered Matt. The police were going to find it even harder to believe. Until she had the proof that would convince them she knew she was vulnerable. Even if J.J. didn't dare break into the house again he could easily find some other way to kill her. She shivered. And no one would know he had done it. No one but her.

Stephie was momentarily jolted out of her thoughts by having to answer roll. But immediately her mind

Janice Harrell

returned to her problem. Perhaps she was too frightened to think clearly, but no matter which angle she approached it from, she got nowhere. She was almost in a daze as she filed out of homeroom with the others. Proof, she thought desperately. *Somehow* she had to get proof.

14

Stephie got home late from school and immediately ran off a fresh copy of the list she had given Dennis. She had left the modem on, she noticed. Irritated with herself, she switched it off. She was so preoccupied these days she would end up brushing her teeth with mousse.

She would have liked to call Dennis and ask him to come over, but what if he read it as a signal that she wanted more from him than friendship? Now that she was weighed down by her terrible knowledge about J.J. she could have used the company but she wasn't up to coping with romantic complications.

The printer spat out one line and then another with a sound like a tearing zipper. When it had finished, she ripped the page off and studied it. The photographs might be gone, but she had studied them so carefully that when she closed her eyes she could visualize them. She hadn't thought they told her anything vital, but J.J. was obviously worried that they had, otherwise he wouldn't have stolen them.

She wondered if the photos were what he'd been after. But, no, he couldn't possibly have realized they would be lying out on her bureau. Grabbing the envelope must have been impulsive, like so much else that he had done. If her bedroom hadn't faced the front so the streetlight seeped through the blinds at night, he might have missed the envelope altogether. She stared at the list of photos. Was there something she was missing?

Suddenly Stephie pushed her chair away from the computer. She was getting nowhere—and she hadn't even started her American history paper, either. She supposed she'd have to ask Mrs. Warner for more time on the grounds she had suffered a trauma when the burglar broke into her house. She smiled wryly. That was certainly a more original excuse than the dog ate my paper. She wasn't sure Mrs. Warner would buy it, anyway.

Stephie's head jerked as she heard the crunch of car wheels on her gravel driveway. She leapt to her feet, forgetting her knee in her agitation. Pain shot through clear up to her hip and made her gasp. Her heart pounding, she limped to her bedroom window and parted the venetian blinds with her fingers. Jordan's red Corvette sat in the driveway. Stephie sighed in relief. She had already decided that if J.J.'s car drove up, she was going to pretend to be gone no matter how much he banged on the door.

She limped out to the front door. "Hi!" Jordan grinned when she opened the door. "I've had it with stupid Mrs. Warner's paper. What do you say we take a break?"

"That sounds good. I was just thinking I might even go to the mall just to be around people." Stephie smiled weakly. "I'm so jumpy since the break-in."

"Oh, yeah," he said casually. "They caught the guy, didn't they?"

Stephie avoided his eyes. "That's what they say. Where's Melissa?" She had begun to look upon Melissa as a permanent accessory to the Corvette.

He made a face. "She's still slogging away on her paper. Want to get an early dinner? We could go get some burgers."

Stephie gave him a grateful look. The only good thing about knowing J.J. was the murderer was that at least she wasn't driving herself crazy being suspicious of everybody she knew. She changed her clothes and made her way carefully down the steps and out to the car. She fell into the passenger seat. "Ouch."

"What's wrong?"

"My knee," she said apologetically.

"You better get it looked at."

"It just takes time to heal." She made a face. "If I'd just remember to be easy on it, but I keep forgetting."

"Is McDonald's okay?"

"Fine. Anyplace. Really."

As they pulled out of the driveway, Jordan launched into a long account of a problem he'd had with his knee the year before after he hurt it in a tennis match. The treatment involved a complicated program of shots, whirlpool baths, and exercises, but she wasn't paying much attention. She felt as if a weight were lifted from her as they drove away from her house. Just for a while she could get away from all the reminders of the case. Maybe she could even quit thinking about it for a while. She wished the burglar hadn't taken those photographs. They were the only solid evidence she had of what had happened the night Matt died, and she was sorry they were gone.

"Melissa said you took those snapshots she got at the party," Jordan said suddenly.

Stephie felt as if he had been reading her mind. Hot color rushed to her face. "She's wrong," she said. "She must have misplaced them."

"That's what I figured. What on earth would you want with Melissa's pictures? Ansel Adams she ain't."

Stephie was quiet as the Corvette sped down Spinnaker Lane and turned onto the main artery off Sunset Avenue. The car was so low she kept having the unpleasant sensation they were going to be sucked under a truck, so she averted her eyes from the road. "Is that all you came over for? To ask me about Melissa's pictures?"

Jordan flashed her a smile. "Nah. I don't need an excuse to want to see you, Stephie."

Suddenly Stephie was embarrassed. Could it be that Jordan was hitting on her? That would be a strange twist. Melissa would never speak to her again.

Jordan stepped on the gas. "You're sort of a lady of mystery these days, aren't you? Since regionals are over and I never see you. And when I do, you've got your head together with Dennis the Menace."

"I like Dennis."

"Is this romance?" He glanced at her curiously.

Stephie flushed a little but said nothing. The fact was she had been avoiding her friends. Until she had felt pretty sure that J.J. was the murderer, she hadn't wanted to be alone with any of them. She would have liked to explain it to Jordan, but she couldn't risk it. Since Matt had died, Jordan and J.J. had become pretty tight. Jordan was obviously grooming J.J. to be his best friend. When the truth came out, Jordan was going to have a second nasty shock, she reflected ruefully.

"I guess I need to see more of my friends," she said in a colorless voice. "It's been hard for me since Matt died."

"You aren't getting weird about this, are you, Stephie?" Jordan's eyes searched her face.

"Stoplight!" she yelled, pointing at it.

He slammed on the brakes. "You've been acting so funny lately."

Maybe it had been a mistake to come out with Jordan. There was so much she couldn't discuss with him. Probably he was right. She had gotten weird. Her whole life these days was taken up with trying to find out who killed Matt. That and trying to stay alive. Nobody would call that normal. She had made herself an outsider in her own group. No wonder she felt so lost and alone.

"McDonald's!" Jordan announced. "This is where we go in and soak up the romantic ambience and you tell me the story of your life."

Stephie lifted herself out of the deep bucket seat. Careful to put her weight on her good knee, she let the car door slam closed behind her and limped toward the entrance. "You already know the story of my life, Jordan."

"We'll have to settle for the romantic ambience then." He pushed the glass door open for her. "Don't you just love the golden arches and all the little pamphlets trying to persuade you that fast-food litter is ecologically correct."

Suddenly Stephie stiffened. J.J. was sitting alone in the brightly lit No Smoking alcove. He bit into a Big Mac and wiped the sauce off his chin with a napkin.

She was mesmerized by the ordinariness of his action. It seemed incredible that he could sit there so calmly eating after what he had done. She read once that the Nazi prison guards who tortured people were ordinary men who acted pretty much like everyone else. But she had never really believed that until now.

"Hey, it's J.J.!" cried Jordan.

"Why don't we get our stuff to go?" suggested Stephie desperately.

"You don't want to go over and say hi to J.J.?"

"Not really." Stephie didn't know what excuse she could use, but she had no intention of going into the No Smoking alcove where J.J. sat. Her flesh recoiled at the very thought.

Jordan grinned. "Rather be alone with me, huh? Perfectly understandable."

After they ordered, Jordan remembered that he needed to get an algebra assignment from J.J. "Let me just go get that," he suggested. "Won't take a minute."

Stephie hastily gathered up the paper bags of hamburgers and drinks. "I'll take these out to the car and meet you there. You better give me the keys."

"It's not locked." Jordan headed for the No Smoking alcove without looking back at her.

Of course it wasn't locked, thought Stephie. That was Jordan all over. Careless. She picked up two bags in each hand. The drinks bag almost slipped and she had to put the bags back up on the counter and get a better grip. Out of the corner of her eye, she saw that Jordan was already happily leaning on the table chatting with J.J.

Stephie bumped the glass door of the restaurant open with one hip and went out to the Corvette. She realized that she had begun to get used to Dennis's solicitude. It was nice when a guy bothered to listen to what you said, and it was nice to be treated as someone special. Too much of the time when she had been going with Matt, she had to make allowances for him. She realized suddenly that she was fed up with making allowances. Yes, she could definitely get used to going with someone as nice as Dennis. She poised the bags on the shiny red hood and opened the car door. Then, grabbing the bags, she lowered herself into the bucket seat, being careful to put her weight only on her good knee. The swivel in was the tricky part, but she managed that, too. Finally she stashed the bags around her feet on the floor.

No need to tell her that Jordan would be talking to J.J. longer than he thought. She had experience with guys talking. Whoever put out the idea that girls were the ones who liked to talk had obviously never seen guys discussing a basketball game. She got a drink from one bag, then fished out the box of chocolate-chip cookies. It was cold in the car, particularly with an iced drink in her hand. Also, she was half-afraid J.J. might sneak away from Jordan and come out after her. Glancing over her shoulder, she checked the door. Mothers, dads, and plenty of kids, but no sign of either J.J. or Jordan.

A beat-up car pulled up just one parking place over. It was Dennis. The last thing she wanted, she realized suddenly, was for Dennis to see her sitting in Jordan's Corvette. Here she had promised faithfully to call him if she needed company and instead she was out with Jordan! This would have to happen just when she had decided she wanted Dennis to like her.

Stephie slid down in the seat hoping to be inconspicuous. It seemed to work. Unfortunately, she dumped the cookies out. A couple of minutes later, when she cautiously got up, she felt a chocolate-chip cookie crunch under her bottom. There were going to be cookie crumbs all over the seat. But at least Dennis hadn't seen her. That was something. She glanced over her shoulder and saw that the glass door was just closing behind him.

Now she had to get up the cookie crumbs. She sighed. Considering the black rag that lay carelessly on the floor of the elegant car, one might argue that to anyone who was as casual about his car as Jordan, a few cookie crumbs here or there made no difference, but Stephie didn't like to think about the cookie being pulverized under her bottom. She twisted around in the seat and began trying to dislodge the cookie crumbs from the deep, sunken seams of the seat. The leather seat was made with six deep seams across the seat, presumably to give it a softer, cushy look. Unfortunately, that meant there were six times as many places for the cookie crumbs to hide. It was amazing how they had got all over the place. Stephie wedged her fingers in one of the leather grooves and groped. Her fingers touched cold metal. Puzzled, she slipped the metal bit out then stared in astonishment at her crumb-encrusted fingers. Between her thumb and index finger she held the key to a Ford.

A Ford? Jordan's family doesn't own a Ford, she thought. The hair at the back of her neck stood on end as an idea slowly floated to the surface of her mind. The truck that had killed Matt was a Ford. That would be just like Jordan, she thought numbly. To run off with the key to the truck after committing murder with it.

A shock of cold swept over her as the driver's door was thrown open. Jordan got in the car and smiled at her wolfishly. "What have you got there?" He leaned toward her and the bead necklace around his neck swung forward, azure and maize and red beads. One of a kind.

"That's Matt's necklace," she choked.

Jordan tucked it under his shirt. "So, I'm an Indian giver." He smiled.

Stephie had remembered what it was about the photographs that had bothered her. The long white curve of Matt's neck in the photograph taken just before he died. Subconsciously, she must have realized something was missing. He had been wearing the necklace when they were in the kitchen together.

"You took it off him because you knew you were going to kill him."

"Let's say I just didn't see any sense in its getting trashed just because Matt was checking out of this life. I mean, heck, it's the real thing. I wanted it back." He fingered the tightly sewn beading complacently. "I guess that might have been the last thing I said to him. 'Let me take care of it for you,' I said. Heck, I don't even think he noticed he was so blitzed."

Her mouth was so dry she couldn't speak. She stared at him unbelievingly. He had murdered Matt! She realized that though she had formally considered Jordan as a suspect, she had never really believed it could have been him. He and Matt had been like brothers!

"Why don't you drop that key down on the floor," he suggested. She heard a click and realized that he had locked the car's power locks. She was trapped.

"You were driving that truck!" she cried.

"Nah!" he said lightly. "I just collect used truck keys."

He pulled out of the parking place so abruptly she was thrown back against the seat. The car bounced over one of the parking lot's speed bumps at such a rate Stephie hoped for a second he had broken an axle. But then, to her surprise, at the back of the almost deserted section of the long parking lot, he slowed down dramatically. The back was where the broad parking lot of McDonald's merged with the parking lot of the Paws Inn Kennel. It was a broad, deserted stretch of black asphalt.

"I'm afraid you are going to have a serious accident." He glanced at her briefly. "Thinking of jumping out? Sure. Go ahead."

Stephie winced a little as her door lock clicked to the open position. She gulped painfully. He had already run over one person. She wondered if, with her bad knee, she could possibly run fast enough to get away before he hit her. And what if her knee gave way and she fell? Sick fear churned in her stomach. Surreptitiously, she glanced around the car. It was a good twenty feet to the edge of the parking lot. She couldn't make it.

"How could you do it?" she screamed. "How could you kill your best friend. Were you drunk?"

He stiffened. "I never get drunk. You know that. Matt was the one who was drunk."

Stephie stared at him, fascinated. At last she would find out exactly what happened, even if she had to die for it because Jordan obviously wanted to talk. He looked directly at her, his dark brows drawn together in a look of intense concentration, as if he were willing her to understand.

"He told me he was going to back out of our trip to Europe." Jordan slapped the steering wheel with his open hand. "We'd been planning it for three years. Had the passports and everything. And you know what he said? He said he was backing out just so he could stop me from going! He knew my parents would never let me go by myself. 'I'm sitting in the catbird seat, now.' That's what he said! He was so drunk he could hardly stand up and he was telling me he was going to control me. He was going to make me dance to his tune. He was sick of tagging along after me, doing what I wanted. He was going to ruin it all for me just to show me he could. Can you believe that?" Jordan stopped talking for a moment and became puzzled. "The thing is, Stephie, in this life there are leaders and there are followers. Matt was born to be a follower. Heck, I *made* that guy. He didn't have a single thought that didn't come from me. He didn't know how to sit, didn't know how to stand, didn't have the first idea about being cool. Man, I helped him. I guided him. And here he is like the monster turning on Frankenstein. From now on he's going to be calling the shots, he said!" Jordan's hand trembled on the beaded necklace. "Who did he think he was, trying to rack up my summer, talking about controlling me!" He choked. "I just completely lost it. I saw red. I did. Really. It was like a red haze. I could feel these blood vessels sort of swelling in my head, like they were going to burst. But somehow I got him outside."

"How did you do that? Matt loved parties. He never wanted to leave."

Jordan looked surprised. "I just told him he had had enough and that I'd better drive him home."

Poor Matt, thought Stephie. No matter what drastic measures he took to get free, he ended up going along with what Jordan said after all. She should have seen that. It had to have been Jordan who got him to leave the party. Nobody else had that kind of influence over him.

"He was a deadweight as I helped him outside,"

Jordan said, making a brief annoyed gesture. "He actually fell asleep leaning against me. I was so disgusted I just let him fall. He was lying there on the driveway, snoring, and it hit me that it would be a really easy thing for somebody to run right over him.

"I guess I was so mad I wasn't thinking straight. I ran along the line of cars, and when I saw the keys in the truck"—he shrugged—"well, it took only a few minutes."

Fear twisted in Stephie's stomach like a knife. He had killed Matt and he was going to kill her. That's why he was talking so freely. They were far back in the parking lot. Probably no one would even see what was happening to her until it was too late.

"When I saw all the blood on the truck and I realized he was really dead, I felt sick. I knew I had gone too far." Jordan sounded faintly aggrieved. "But he shouldn't have got me so mad. He really pushed me, Stephie. He only had himself to blame. Okay, get out of the car."

"No!"

"Oh, all right. Have it your way. It was a mistake," Jordan said calmly. "I admit that. You wouldn't believe how many times I've wished Matt were still around. I miss him! You know that? But I'm not going to let one stupid mistake ruin my whole life."

Stephie's head jerked as the car charged forward and zipped out of the parking lot. Stephie hastily pulled her seat belt across her chest and fastened it.

The motor growled viciously as they raced the short distance down Beal Street, Jordan swiftly shifting gears. He ran the red light and then turned onto Sunset. Brakes screeched and horns blared as cars braked desperately to avoid the streaking Corvette.

"They're going to remember your car," Stephie said dully.

"You'd be surprised at what people can't remember." Jordan smiled.

Stephie took a deep shuddering breath. "Well, I hear what you're saying, Jordan. You made a mistake, but that's over and done with. Now that I know what happened, well—let's just forget the whole thing. I understand. Really."

He chuckled. "Nice try. But I don't believe you. You've been poking around right from the beginning trying to find out what happened. I tried to warn you off but you wouldn't listen. You can't make me believe you're going to let this slide after all this. I don't like doing this, Stephie, but I'm not going to let you foul up my life."

He was frowning, thinking hard as they sped along Sunset. Suddenly Stephie realized she didn't want to wait to see what "accident" he was thinking up for her. She grabbed the steering wheel and twisted it toward her. Jordan jabbed her hard with his elbow but it was too late. The car was already leaping the curb. Lurching wildly over a parking curb, it crashed against the brick side of the Pizza Hut with a sickening jolt and the brief, loud, implacable crunch of a car hitting brick. Stephie's teeth rattled. For a minute or two she sat stunned in the leather seat, listening to the tinkle of falling glass. The headlights had disintegrated on contact.

She was alive. That was all that mattered. She looked at the empty seat beside her. Jordan must have gone through the windshield, she thought vaguely. The windshield was gone, too. It lay in odd-shaped marbles all over the long shiny hood.

"Is he breathing?" someone yelled. "Call an ambulance. And call the cops."

The cops, Stephie thought muzzily. Right. I have something to tell the cops. But right at the moment she felt too cold and tired to do anything. "You okay?" somebody called.

Dennis suddenly appeared beside her and jerked her car door open. "My God, I thought it looked like Jordan's car," he panted. "We heard the crash down at McDonald's. Are you okay?"

Stephie heard a siren in the distance. "Jordan—" she began.

"Don't worry about Jordan," he said hastily. "Somebody just told me the ambulance is on the way."

Suddenly Stephie remembered what she had to show the police. She fumbled in the pocket of her jeans then held out the key to Dennis with a smile.

"What's that?" He helped her out of the car. "We better get you away from the car," he said, eyeing it nervously. "Sometimes they explode."

They sat down together on the curb of the walkway of the restaurant. A couple of men had laid their coats over Jordan. His face was bloody. "Is he dead?" Stephie asked with mild interest.

"No, no," said Dennis hastily. "Nothing like that. Don't worry."

J.J. had been kneeling beside Jordan, but one glance at Stephie and he stripped off his jacket, came over, and wrapped it around her shoulders. "She's in shock," he said briefly. "You're supposed to keep them warm." He glanced back at Jordan, but now their view of him was blocked by emergency personnel with a rolling stretcher. "I guess I'd better call Jordan's mom, don't you think? Or maybe I'd better go get her and drive her to the hospital." He shook his head. "Jeez, Stephie, how did it happen?"

Stephie held out the key.

"What's that?"

"I've got something to show the police!" she said brightly.

"Maybe you ought to put your head down between your legs," said Dennis.

"I'm making perfect sense," she said indignantly. "Jordan tried to kill me. He was going to run me over with the Corvette, and *this*"—she held the key aloft—"this is the key to the truck that he used to kill Matt!"

J.J. sat down suddenly on the curb.

"Are you *sure*, Stephie?" asked Dennis earnestly.

"You are looking at proof, fella!"

"Maybe," J.J. said, "I'll just hold off for a while on calling Jordan's mom."

Epilogue

I was so dumb." Stephie picked up a piece of pizza and considered it gloomily. She realized now that she had been insane to trust her instincts. She would never make that mistake again. Cold reason was more dependable. Sure, she got goose bumps when J.J. said "damn," but obviously her unconscious mind wasn't reacting to his voice, but simply to the single word.

Dennis patted her hand. "You weren't dumb. We were the dumb ones."

Stephie was sitting at the edge of the booth because her knee was now wrapped in an elaborate beige contraption with straps, and she needed room to dangle it off the side of the bench. Her crutch was propped against the booth. "I don't know," she said. "I sure feel pretty dumb. I got in the car with him, didn't I?"

Melissa sat with a pink and swollen face in the corner and dabbed at her eyes with a tissue. "Eat!"

Rachel commanded her, pushing a slice of pizza toward her.

Stephie noted with interest that Rachel was wearing a pink sweater. She wondered if the black was going to be phased out gradually or if Goodwill Industries was about to receive half a truckload of used clothing suitable for wearing by the deeply depressed.

"You think you know people!" Melissa clumsily blew her nose.

Stephie waited for Rachel to say something like "I told you so," but it didn't happen. Rachel was evidently drawing on reserves of tact Stephie never knew she had. She didn't rub it in that she had been right about Jordan.

Of all of them, Sumir was the only one eating heartily. He had heaped his plate with three kinds of pizza from the buffet table plus a thin slice of the chocolate-chip variety for dessert. "I hope you're going to explain this a little better, Stephie. It still seems pretty strange to me. Murder!"

"Jordan's parents say it's all a mix-up," said J.J. "They're hiring a big-shot defense attorney from New York."

"It'll be interesting to see how he explains the truck key," said Stephie.

Sumir shook his head. "I can't understand why he kept it."

"He probably didn't even know he had it," said Stephie. "He just absentmindedly stuck it in his pocket. I expect he was pretty rattled—and then somehow it fell out and got stuck in the seat cushion."

Melissa sniffled loudly.

"Come on, Melissa," Rachel said. "Let's go splash some cold water on that face and you'll feel better."

They watched the two girls make their way toward the ladies' room. "I know it's good for Melissa to get out of the house and all," said Dennis, "but she sure does cast a damper on the party."

"I don't feel so great myself, if you want to know the truth." J.J.'s mouth twisted. "You could have knocked me over with a feather. Jordan!"

"That's what I can't figure out," said Sumir, looking mystified. "He had it all—car, girl, grades. He would have looked *great* on a college application. And he threw it away."

"Well, naturally, you couldn't understand it," said Dennis. "You're completely different from Jordan."

"You bet I am! And let me tell you I resent the comparison."

"Dennis just means that if you ever committed a murder, it would be a different kind of murder," explained Stephie. "I kick myself that I didn't realize that this one had Jordan's fingerprints all over it. Jordan is so quick. Impulsive, really."

"Like the way he kept ringing in with the Quiz Bowl answers before they even finished reading the question. I should have remembered that," said Dennis.

"Lots of times he got the right answer, though," pointed out Sumir.

"Yeah, and he was vain about it," said Dennis. "He was really proud that he could ring in so fast. Act first, think later, that's his style. And like Stephie said, he was careless."

"Like with the key," said Sumir.

"Like with everything," said Stephie. "He never locked his locker, remember? And he didn't bother to take care of that fancy car of his. I think he figured things would take care of themselves, as if he *deserved* for things to go right. I don't think he ever thought anything bad would happen to him. Maybe that was why he was so shocked when Matt turned against him."

Rachel came back to the table by herself, looking grim. "Melissa's going on home," she said. "She says she just can't face food yet." As Rachel scooted back into her seat, everyone watched silently. "Well, I offered to go with her," Rachel said defensively, "but she said she's okay to drive. Besides I want to hear what happened."

"We could sit here all night," J.J. said heavily. "And it still wouldn't make sense to me."

"I told you Jordan had a terrible temper, didn't I?" said Rachel smugly. "I told you he was self-centered and immature. Personally, I was afraid of him. That night at regionals when I hit him, I could feel myself curdling inside." She opened her eyes wide. "I mean, did you see his face?"

"Matt never wanted to cross him either," Stephie said. "Looking back, I think that was why Matt got so drunk. He was working himself up to breaking off with Jordan and he didn't think he could do it sober. It wasn't that he was afraid of him." Stephie rearranged the pizza crusts on her plate. "It's just that they were so close. Matt had always tagged along after Jordan and let him call the shots. He didn't like doing that but he couldn't quite help himself. They were really good friends and Jordan was such a dominant sort of person."

"Yeah," said J.J., "but when Matt had you to hang around with, he didn't need Jordan so much."

"I don't know about that." Stephie fiddled with her silverware. "All I know is he was getting tremendously worked up about being independent. It was tough for him to break off that friendship with Jordan, but for some reason he felt he had to, and the only way he could make himself do it was to get really drunk and nasty."

"Then Jordan completely lost it and killed him," put in Sumir.

"Yes." Stephie frowned. "I think Jordan realized that Matt wasn't *just* drunk. Those things he was saying—that he was sick of Jordan calling the shots, that he was going to be boss now, that he was going to ruin everything for Jordan—those were things he really meant."

"He wouldn't have been able to stick to them, though," said J.J. "You know the way Matt was."

Stephie sighed. "Probably not."

J.J. shook his head. "I can see how Jordan might temporarily lose control and kill Matt. But the burglary—that's different. It was cold-blooded and it was stupid, besides. What did he think he was going to do?"

"Kill me, probably," said Stephie bleakly.

"You're kidding!"

"I'm not. Do you happen to know if Jordan owned a gun?"

"He did, actually. A little automatic his uncle gave him when his uncle got into big guns. But—" J.J. shook his head helplessly. "I just can't believe he'd shoot you down in cold blood."

"I don't know why you're so surprised at that," Dennis said. "You know he threatened to run her down with the Corvette."

"Yeah, but somehow that's different."

Remembering the awful night of the burglary, Stephie felt almost sick. She had to remind herself that she was safe now. Jordan was in the hospital and when he got out, he would go to jail. "He was probably hoping to get the photographs back, too," she added. "I'm sure Melissa told Jordan I had stolen that packet of snapshots she took at the party."

"Well, for heaven's sake," snapped Rachel, "she never dreamed he was going to try to murder you to get them back."

"Oh, I know that," Stephie said. "I'm just mad at myself for not seeing how it all fit together. I should have guessed it was Jordan when the photographs came up missing after the burglary. Who else would Melissa have talked to about the missing photos? She wasn't likely to go all over school saying 'Stephie stole my snapshots.' That would sound too silly, even for Melissa. But she probably told Jordan. I'll bet she told him everything. And he must have figured they were important or he wouldn't have grabbed them in a blind panic when the alarm went off. I think he didn't like it that the photos showed he was the last person to be with Matt before he died." She frowned suddenly. "Though I can't think how he could have known about that."

"Didn't you have all that stuff on your computer?" suggested Dennis.

"That's right! He could have tapped into it." Stephie put her face in her hands. "I guess I'm not cut out to be a detective."

"Well, you got the goods on him. Nobody else did."

Stephie smiled ruefully. "I wasn't exactly brilliant, was I? Seems like I was just bumbling along. But I was doing enough to worry him. He didn't like it that I was nosing around trying to find evidence. He had just killed Matt on the spur of the moment, so probably he wasn't sure he had covered his tracks real well. He was counting on its passing as an accident, and nobody would do any real investigating. But when I told everybody that I was looking for Matt's killer, it scared him."

"Well, I didn't like Jordan much," said Rachel, "but I sure never thought he was a murderer. Never."

"He wasn't a murderer to begin with. But something just snapped inside him," said Stephie. "Matt pushed him too far. Matt was too drunk to see the danger signals, I guess. He just sat there taunting Jordan until he reached a kind of flashpoint. He told me he was so mad he literally couldn't see. After that, everything he did was just a matter of covering his tracks."

"Yeah, you obviously were making him nervous," said Dennis.

"I was the only one who was sure Matt had been murdered. And I was weird about it. I wasn't going to give up and Jordan knew that."

"Well, you better take good care of yourself," said Dennis. "You're the chief witness."

"As long as they don't let him out on bail, I ought to be okay." Stephie smiled a little. "Anyway, my mom will probably never let me out of her sight after this."

"But she's on the road most of the time, isn't she?" asked J.J.

"Not anymore. She's put in for a job back at her old office. Our plan is to sell the house and move into a smaller apartment."

"That's too bad!" said Rachel. "That neat view you have and all!"

"I don't mind that. I've sort of developed this thing." Stephie looked down and stirred her tea with a straw. "It's funny but I just don't like big glass windows anymore."

"What you like now is a few tasteful iron bars on the

windows?" Dennis grinned and Stephie smiled back at him happily.

"If you didn't suspect Jordan, Stephie, who did you suspect?" asked Sumir. "You must have figured somebody did it."

Her eyes strayed unwillingly to J.J.

"Come on!" J.J. protested. "You didn't!"

"Not really," Stephie lied. "But you had been acting pretty strange lately. Like the way you pushed me in the hall the other day."

J.J.'s face reddened. "Yeah, but it's just that I've had a lot on my mind." He hesitated, then seemed to make a sudden decision to speak. "Fact is, I found out I've got this problem. I mean, I went in for all these tests and they say I've got diabetes." His voice grew hoarse. "I just don't know what it's going to mean yet. The guy here didn't seem all that sure. My parents have made an appointment for me with this sports medicine expert. Then—we'll see. But I can't get in to see him for another week." He clenched his fist. "I'm just about going out of my mind."

"Oh, diabetes is nothing," said Rachel blithely. "My aunt has it. You just watch what you eat and take your medicine and that's all there is to it."

J.J. regarded her with cold disdain, but didn't bother to point out that as her aunt was not an Olympic aspirant her problems were not exactly comparable to his.

Well, that explained why J.J. had been acting so strange, Stephie thought sympathetically. He had a pressure cooker going inside him. And to think she had even considered trying to sneak into Matt's house to search his room for evidence against J.J.!

"It's going to be different without Jordan around."

J.J. blinked. "I wonder what's going to happen to him. Fact is, I guess I haven't quite taken it all in yet."

Stephie felt she hadn't exactly absorbed what had happened either. Suddenly Jordan was out of the picture and everything felt different. Finished. More peaceful. She reflected that other big changes were coming up. It was going to be a change moving into a little apartment and having her mother around all the time, clucking over her and worrying about her. Mrs. Yates had been truly shaken when she realized how close Stephie had come to getting killed.

Stephie wasn't kidding herself that it was going to be easy to testify against Jordan, particularly with some hotshot lawyer cross-examining her.

She looked around the table affectionately. Her friends weren't all perfect, that was for sure. But they were familiar and comforting, steady in a confusing time.

"We ought to toast Stephie," said Dennis. "Let's face it, she more or less singlehandedly brought Jordan to justice and at considerable risk to herself."

"You don't toast with iced tea," said Rachel.

"I don't see why not," said Dennis.

They raised their plastic iced tea glasses. "Cheers!" said Sumir.

"You should toast with champagne or something," grumbled Rachel. "That's not what I call a real toast."

Stephie smiled. Rachel being Rachel—there was something comfortable about that, too.

Later, as they left Pizza Hut, Dennis put his arm around Stephie and walked her to her car. "So, how are you feeling?" he asked anxiously.

"Honestly, Dennis, I am not falling apart so quit asking me. Except for this stupid contraption on my knee, I'm fine."

"Sure?"

"Sure. All ghosts are laid to rest." She smiled up at him and he bent to kiss her. "Watch out! Don't step on my contraption," Stephie warned. "Golly, I'll be glad when I'm out of this thing."

"I think it's kind of cute." Dennis smiled goofily and squeezed her tight.

"Good." Stephie laughed softly. At last, she thought, it was time for starting over.

About the Author

Janice Harrell decided she wanted to be a writer when she was in the fourth grade. She grew up in Florida and received her master's and doctorate degrees in eighteenth-century English literature from the University of Florida. After teaching college English for a number of years, she began to write full time.

She lives in Rocky Mount, North Carolina, with her husband, a psychologist, and their daughter. Ms. Harrell is a compulsive traveler—some of the countries she has visited are Greece, France, Egypt, Italy, England, and Spain—and she loves taking photographs.